Angels Can Laugh Too

THE CHRONICLES OF A GUARDIAN ANGEL

Angels Can Laugh Too

THE CHRONICLES OF A GUARDIAN ANGEL

BY ALBERTA ROTHE NIELSON

CFI
SPRINGVILLE, UTAH

ISBN: 1-55517-827-8
e. 1

Published by CFI
An Imprint of Cedar Fort Inc.
www.cedarfort.com

Distributed by:

Typeset by Natalie Roach
Cover design by Nicole Shaffer
Cover design © 2004 by Lyle Mortimer

Printed in the United States of America
10 9 8 7 6 5 4 3 2 1
Printed on acid-free paper

Library of Congress Cataloging-in-Publication Data

Nielson, Alberta Rothe, 1929-
   Angels can laugh too : the chronicles of a guardian angel / by Alberta Rothe
Nielson.-- 1st ed.
        p. cm.
   Includes bibliographical references (p.   ).
   ISBN 1-55517-827-8 (acid-free paper)
 1. Guardian angels--Fiction.   I. Title.

   PS3614.I364A84 2004
   813'.6--dc22

2004022740

Dedication

To my children:
Toi, Rico, Ray, Peggy, Guy, Victoria, Ed—
they are my jewels.

Foreword

Why should you read this book?

Since September 11, 2001, we need positive stories and literature to help us cope with this "new world" we live in today. People of the world are in need of, and are beginning to search for something to give them hope, something to lift their spirits, and something to cling to when there are problems around them. Having faith that there could be promptings and guidance in their daily lives from an unseen force gives them this hope. It could be Karma, a Higher Power, Luck, or even an Angel; just something that whispers to their conscience and gives them guidance and peace.

When this gentle unseen helper whispers to the conscience, an idea just pops up in your mind. You wonder where it came from. Perhaps it may be a warning to protect you or your family from harm, or perhaps it may be as simple as help deciding between a right and a wrong action or choice.

This little book is easy reading. It will make you laugh, wonder, and even cry a little. Read it to your children. Put it in your teenager's backpack. Keep it on the coffee table. What happens when a prompting is followed or ignored? Herein are lessons for all ages to learn. Enjoy.

Table of Contents

Prologue   ix

1   BUT MOM . . .   1

2   THE LAST TRAIN RIDE   7

3   GOLDEN DAFFODIL MAGIC   19

4   WHO ARE YOU?   25

5   FOR THE GOOD OF THE CHILDREN   29

6   PLEASE STOP THE WIND   39

7   ALL IS NOT LOST   45

8   TALK ABOUT LUCK!   55

9   THE MIRACLE OF SPRING   69

10 PUSH, PUSH, MAKE TEARS   75

11 LEMON AND LIME   81

12 OPPOSITION   85

Epilogue   95

Bibliography   99

About the Author   102

Prologue

Facts do not cease to exist
because they are ignored.
—ANONYMOUS

I used to wonder if there were angels. Sometimes brilliant thoughts would pop into my mind and I would wonder where they came from. My mother would say, "Your guardian angel told you that."

"Are there such things?" I asked her.

"I believe that there are angels around us."[1]

"Have you seen them?"

"No, I have not seen them, but sometimes when I am very happy or very sad I feel a presence and wonder if they are really there. Just believing that they could be there gives me comfort and helps me to be a better person."

My mother was right—guardian angels do exist. I know because now I am one, and the transition from mortal to angel was, if I might jest, a once-in-a-lifetime experience . . .

My grandson Eddy and I were on the golf course. It was a nice summer day, perhaps too warm, because I suddenly felt a little faint. A salty drop of moisture fell into my eye and I realized my forehead was damp and clammy. I wiped the drip away with my sleeve and teed off. By the time I reached my ball my knees were weak and my breath was short. I told Eddy that I just had to sit down a minute. The grass felt so cool that I stretched right out, full length.

"Are you alright, Grandpa?" Eddy asked as he sat down beside me. I could see the concerned look on his face.

"Just feel a little weak is all. Maybe it's too hot for an old duffer like me."

"Let's just rest awhile, Grandpa. We only have two holes to finish." We chatted until a call from the group behind moved us on. Eddy picked up my clubs and said, "That's enough for today, Grandpa. Let's go."

My yearly visit to see Eddy and his family in Boulder, Colorado was always a highlight of my retired life. Our golf game was going so well, bonding grandfather and grandson closer together. As I drove home, Eddy directed the way, but he didn't take me to his home—he led me straight to the emergency door at the hospital.

Yes, I remember now, that is where I was—in a bed at the hospital. That was my heartbeat on the monitor. "What is this thing in my nose?" I whispered.

"That's oxygen, Grandpa." It was Eddy's voice. "How do you feel?"

"I don't know—kinda funny."

"Is that funny haha or funny peculiar?" he teased.

I smiled. This is quite a grandson I have.

"Grandpa, I'm going to phone Dad; I'll be back in a minute."

I heard his footsteps as he left. He is a bright boy

for a twelve-year-old.

A bright light on the ceiling caught my eye. It looked like a hole right in the corner of the room. *That is strange,* I thought. *Why would there be a hole up there in the corner?* I looked out the window; the sun was shining brightly, but the light coming from the hole was much brighter than the sunshine.

"Hi, Grandpa. I'm back." Eddy's voice cut into my thoughts. His red eyes and flushed face told me that he must have been crying. I guess he was worried about his old grandpa.

"Did you get a hold of your dad?" I asked.

"Yes. He'll be here soon."

Eddy sat close to the side of my bed and laid his hand on my arm. With my eyes half open I could see him study the tubes and wires that were hooked up to me. Reaching up, he put my greying curly locks back in place. Then he did the craziest thing—my Eddy licked his thumb and finger and smoothed my mustache in the same motion as I do it. I smiled. Yes, he is quite a kid, but I was more interested in that bright light up in the corner of the room.

What is it? I wondered, and the next thing I knew I was right up there looking at it. It felt so light and airy to be floating around, circling this way and that. A most peaceful aura seemed to surround me. I looked down and realized that it was me in the bed, and Eddy was sitting there with his head resting on my arm. *How could this be?* I thought. *That is me down there, and this is me up here.*

The bright light caught my eye again and seemed to beckon me like a magnet. The closer I got to the hole and the light, the closer I wanted to be to it.

Suddenly I swished right through it.[2]

I found myself standing in front of a extraordinarily kind looking man. His flowing robe was as white as his beautiful head of hair. A choir was singing. *What beautiful voices—just like angels,* I thought.

"Where am I?" I whispered. I felt as if I was in a void. Then it came to me. I was in a bed—a hospital bed. That is where the bed was—in the hospital—and I was in it. I could hear my heartbeat on a monitor.

Oh yes, I remember. The words came back to me now. "Where is my grandson?"

A kind, soft voice spoke to me. "Your name is Randolf Rippenhoffer?"

"Yes sir," I answered.

"But better known as R Squared?"

"Yes sir," I answered with a grin, pleased that my nickname was known, even here. Wherever 'here' is.

My mind wandered back to where 'R Squared' began. At first my friends called me RR for short, for Randolf Rippenhoffer. Then we learned in our math class that RR can mean R times R and is written with a little ^{2} above it (R^2), pronounced "R squared." It was easier to say "R Squared" than "Randolph Rippenhoffer."

"OK R^2," the man said with a chuckle, and then his voice became serious. "You have finished your mortal time on earth."

He must have seen the surprised look on my face, for he added, "Yes, this is Heaven." A hot flush passed through my whole being in confirmation of his words. He continued, "Your records show that you have performed very well during your stay there. Yes, you have bent the rules sometimes, and done some unworthy acts, but I am pleased to inform you that you have done your best to make them right. Your greatest blessing from heaven has been your gift of freedom to choose right or wrong. That was the test while you were mortal, to choose the right instead of the wrong. But you are no longer a mortal. Now you are in a new stage of your progression. And I have a new assignment for you."

That caught my attention. *Isn't this a place of peace and rest?* I thought.

His voice broke into my thoughts, "Yes, this is a place of peace and rest. You will find peace and rest in your new assignment. You have been a very successful family man. There is a great need of your experience on earth to help build better family relationships. The family is the most sacred unit ever created," he explained. "It is in trouble now. The forces of evil are penetrating the very foundation of family unity."[3]

My mind wandered back to experiences I had had on earth. I also thought of some of the sad situations and circumstances I had witnessed: I saw split families, struggling single mothers, lonesome grandfathers, neglected babies, rag-a-muffin children, empty cupboards, and full prisons—all causing buckets of tears. The thoughts continued to flood through my mind like a motion picture show. *Yes, the family unit is struggling for survival,* I thought.

"R^2," he called. "R^2, I can see what you are thinking." My inner picture show faded as he continued. "You are right. Those things are the results of families in trouble. Do you agree?"

I nodded my head.

"Would you like, as your assignment, to be of help in situations like these?" Then he looked deep into my eyes, and added, "R^2, would you like to be a Guardian Angel?"[4]

I stared at him. *Are there such things?* I thought.

Again, he read my mind. "Yes, there are such things."

Then my mother was right.

"Yes, your mother was right." His words echoed my thoughts. "Mortals are very vulnerable during their passage on earth. Guardian angels are there to help and guide them, if mortals will only listen to the promptings . . ."

Right there I dropped out of the conversation. My mind was remembering at the speed of light. *Someone was there watching me all of the time? Someone could see all of my foibles? Whew!*

The man laughed. He knew what I was thinking.

I was surprised to hear him laugh, so he added, "Heaven is a happy place. We have emotions here just like mortals.[5] Now, what about that assignment we were talking about? Would you like to be a Guardian Angel?"

"Yes, yes I would."

He continued, "Remember that you are new at this. Do not feel that you can solve every problem. It takes time and experience to accomplish the things you need to do. Be patient with yourself."

I nodded in understanding.

He paused, then added, "There are some rules you need to be aware of."

"Yes Sir?"

"You will not be seen, only your presence felt."

"Then how can I influence them?" I asked.

"You can put an idea into the mind to help them make good choices," he replied.

"But what if they will not listen?"

"You can sort of . . . bug them; make them feel nervous, so they get jittery; or you can mix up their thinking and then give them a new thought."

"I can do that?"

"Of course you can," he encouraged. "But you will also find those who have not learned to listen, or who will not listen. Sometimes a conscience is so heavy with guilt it cannot be reached."

"What do I do then?" I asked.

"It takes a lot of patience on your part to develop an insight into the cause of the deeds. Remember that it is not the person that is bad, it is the deed. You will find that with practice you will develop the skill to separate the deed from the doer."

I sat there in silence, thinking of the challenge he had placed before me.

"You can also help them to feel pleased with themselves as a reward for doing good."

"I love it!" I cried out, hardly able to contain myself.

He smiled. "One more thing—I ask you to keep a record of your contacts and experiences.[6] All of these things, as you know by now, must be recorded in Heaven."[7]

"Yes, I know that now, and I will keep a record." Then I had a thought and asked, "May I leave my signature at each case number?"

"You want to write Randolf Rippenhoffer?" he

chuckled.

I smiled. "No Sir, it will be R^2 written in the most inconspicuous places."

"You may have your wish. Now go, work with families and individuals. Make a difference for good in their lives."

"Thank you, Sir, thank you very much." Again, a rapid wave of heat coursed through my being and warmed me to the very pit of my heart.

"And remember R^2," he added with a smile, "Be of good cheer because . . . ANGELS CAN LAUGH TOO."

1

*Do not think it wasted time
to submit yourself to any influence
that will bring upon you any noble feeling.*
—RUSKIN

BUT MOM . . .

I dropped into a kitchen on Salem Street. I can do that, you know, because I am an angel. A mother was seriously quizzing a small boy of about five years of age. "Rayman, are you chewing gum?" The boy nodded his tousled blonde head up and down as his small fist tightened around the remaining gum in his pocket.

"Where did you get it?" she continued. Rayman ducked his head and put his hand over his freckled nose as if to hide his guilt, then shrugged his shoulders in answer.

"Look at me," his mother said as she lifted his chin up and looked straight into his blue eyes. "Now where did you get that gum?"

"At the store," came his cautious answer in a quiet guarded voice. Rayman knew that he was in trouble. The gum in his pocket was still in his closed fist and all of a sudden he wished it was not there.

"Did you pay for it?" The boy shook his head back and forth causing the dammed up tears to spill down his freckled cheeks.

"Well, you better not do that again," she said, grabbing both of his shoulders in a shake, "or I will put the wooden spoon to your bottom."

Stop that, I called into her mind. *Don't shake him.* She stopped. I could see that she was stunned, that she didn't quite know where the warning had come from. *Shaking your son like that can damage his tender brain.*

The mother turned back to the stove where their dinner was simmering. She didn't know why, but my message to her conscience made her very nervous. Without thinking she picked up the hot lid in her bare hands. When the lid hit the floor, Rayman ran. When his mother turned around, he was gone.

Surveying her burned fingers, his mother slumped down onto the kitchen stool, but I kept the boy in her mind. "Rayman shouldn't do that," she mumbled to herself, "He knows better. You just don't go picking things up like that. I should take him back to the store, but that would be so embarrassing."

I bugged her with the thoughts of her grown boy ending up in jail if he wasn't stopped now. With that picture in mind she turned off the burner and quickly moved to find her son.

Rayman was in his room nonchalantly playing with his cars as if nothing had happened. Observing these actions, his mother could tell that picking up the gum without paying for it didn't seem to be too big a deal to him after all.

"Where is that gum?" Rayman jumped with surprise when he heard his mother's voice. He pulled the package from his pocket, but there was only one stick left. The rest was a large gob in his mouth. I cautioned her to be gentle so she sat on the floor beside him. "I am not pleased that you took gum without paying for it. You know that isn't right. Don't you?" Her calm voice surprised him and I could see repentance seeping into his face.

He nodded in agreement.

"What do you think we should do about it?" she asked. His shoulders shrugged again as more tears formed.

I whispered to him, *YOU have money.* His face brightened when he realized that he could solve the problem. "I have some money in my jar," he said, looking up at his mother for approval.

"Then go get it," she encouraged, still inwardly dreading the embarrassment of having to go to the store.

We watched him as he climbed onto his chair, onto the dresser, and two steps across the dresser to the open clothes' closet. Stretching his chubby body as far as it would reach, he brought a jar down from the very top shelf.

The coins jingled as he grabbed a handful. He struggled to get his hand out of the jar and had to drop a few coins in the process. His mother smiled as she watched the pudgy fingers count out the pennies. *Yes, this is the right thing to do,* she thought.

"Now let's go," she said as she smiled and reached down for his hand which was still full of coins. Rayman shoved them into his pocket and reached for his mother's hand. Together they went out the door to walk the three blocks to the store. I followed them.

When they reached the store, Rayman stopped at the door and pulled his hand away from his mother's. "I don't wanna go in there."

Whoops, I thought. *The boy is losing faith in this venture. Watch out, Mother. He may run.*

The mother stopped and put her hand on his shoulder. "I know that facing the store manager is difficult but what you did was not right. You must apologize to the man and pay him for the gum." She reached for Rayman's hand and held it more firmly this time.

"I don't wanna go in there," he said again, trying to pull away from her.

The mother tightened her grip. "I will be with you all of the time."

"I DON'T WANNA GO IN THERE," he shouted while being half dragged through the open door of the store.

They were met by the plump manager who balanced a pencil behind his ear where the hair was getting quite thin. He recognized the situation right away from the mother's embarrassed look and the boy's frightened eyes. The man took them into his secluded office and sat in his big chair. With his kindest smile he said, "Now what can I do for you, son?"

The boy was terrified even with that kind smile there close to his face. *What might he do to me?* the boy wondered. *I don't like this feeling. Wish I didn't take that old gum. It wasn't that good anyway.* He pulled the last stick from his pocket and gave it to the man.

Rayman's tongue was thick and heavy, so heavy that he couldn't move it, so his mother spoke up and

said, "Now tell the man that you are sorry."

"'msorry," he mumbled.

"Give the man your money," she urged. Rayman's hand disappeared deep into his pocket again and came out with the coins. They jingled as he dropped them into the manager's hand.

"Thank you, son," he said with a smile as he gently patted Rayman's shoulder. "Paying for the gum is the right thing to do." Then he sent a nod and a wink to the mother to let her know that she, too, had done the right thing.

Gaily holding hands this time, the mother and son left the store. On the walk home the mother asked, "Are you ever going to do that again?"

"NO WAY," he shouted out, waving his arm in the air.

"Now we are through with that. Don't you feel better?"

"Yes . . . but NO."

"Why do you say no? You have done a very brave thing. You have learned a very important lesson."

Rayman stopped walking, put his free hand up in disgust and yelled, "BUT MOM, IT WAS THE WRONG STORE."[8]

Angels can laugh, and I laughed.

I left my R^2 on Rayman's money jar to remind him that it is best to be honest in all we do.

2

To live in hearts we leave behind is not to die.
—ANONYMOUS

THE LAST TRAIN RIDE 9

I was pleased with my first encounter; pleased that I could really influence another's actions for good. I licked my finger and thumb to smooth my mustache and then gave both ends a twirl. I was drawing my fingers across my lips to put those renegade hairs back into place, when a sign caught my eye:

WARNING!
Jews! Do not report for resettlement!
It's the Death Camp!
Hide! Hide!

It was a terrible thing, an abominable thing. Thousands of Jews were being sent to the death camp gas chambers. I saw thousands hiding in unlighted stoves and packing crates, under dusty floors and over attic spaces, lying flat on roof tops, and standing upright in outhouse stench. Many were children. I saw thousands of parentless children, one hundred of

7

them, in the orphanage run by Boris Pilsudski, whom the children called Uncle Boris.

He was a square-shouldered man with big hands. His face was round and flushed; his eyes were blue and wise. Those eyes gave people an instant feeling of acceptance. He was the right person for a job like this. The children adored him.

I arrived at Boris's orphanage just as he received orders to prepare the children to be resettled to a new orphanage. Because of the warning sign, he knew that it was a train ride to the death camp. The warning sign said to hide, but how could he hide them? There were too many. He had always hoped that perhaps the children would be spared. Into his office he called the two head teachers, known to the children as Aunt Rachel and Aunt Gretta. "The time has finally come," he said. Gretta gasped and Rachel stiffened.

"The Camp?" they said in unison.

Boris nodded, showing the obvious pain in every part of his body. His shoulders stooped as if the breath had gone completely out of him, his hands wrapped around and around each other trying to find a stable grip, and his eyes were clouded with fear for the children.

"Can we take them up the ladder and out over the roof?" asked Rachel.

"All hundred of them?" Boris responded. "And if we did, where could we hide them? Some of them are so small that it would be difficult to keep them quiet. One by one they would be flushed out."

"This is so terrible. So awful for such little ones," Gretta sobbed.

Boris continued, "I understand that we are to think

8

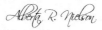

that the children will be herded into a train headed for a new orphanage, but I know that it is the death camp where they will be forced into the gas chamber."

"And burned in that furnace with the big stack," Gretta added.

"Boris, how can we tell the children?" Rachel needed some help so I stepped in to influence her thinking. *Tell the children that we are riding a train to the country to have a picnic.* Her dark-brown eyes registered the prompt. Rachel turned to Gretta and suggested the picnic idea.

Gretta spoke up, and I could see that she had a plan. "I will make them some special candy for a treat. I have a good chocolate recipe." The thought of a picnic in the country with a chocolate treat should be a happy one, but Gretta could hardly speak the words because she knew what was going to be in that chocolate treat. Her mind pictured that bottle, with the skull and cross-bones, far back on her shelf. She had bought it and saved it for such a time as this.

Oh no, I caught my breath, *I know what she is planning to do. Is that right? Should I stop her? Oh this is terrible! What should I do? But then, the children, the children won't suffer.*

"What a great idea Gretta." It was Rachel. She had no idea what Gretta was planning. She quickly put her arms around her friend, and Boris circled them both in his arms.

"When the final notice comes we will get the children together and have a great time," Rachel commented as she dried her eyes. "For now we must continue as if nothing happened."

I did not have to remind Boris that his children

were special. His big heart was full of love for them. He had done all he could do. He had done his very best. Boris wiped his eyes on his sleeve and said, "Love the children all that you can and tell the other workers of our plans. We must make the last days of the children as happy and as loving as they can be."

Gretta busied herself making chocolates; drop by drop her salty tears were stirred into the mixture. Her grey-streaked hair was tied up in a neat ball at the nape of her neck. She always wore it that way during the day to keep it out of her way, but at bedtime she would take out the long hair pins and let it fall down around her shoulders. Her husband had loved it that way. She could still feel his warm breath as he nuzzled her neck through the soft curls. He was gone now. Where? She didn't know. As an able bodied man he had been taken from their home. That was over a year ago. Oh how she missed him.

"So now it has come to this," she muttered to herself. "Has our God let this war go so far as to take the little ones too? A train-car filled with them? I do not understand; how can they hate us so?" Her tears continued to flow as she stirred and stirred. "This special mixture will be sweet to the taste and the children will gently fall asleep."

Days at the orphanage seemed to be happier now. The children blossomed under the added love and attention from their teachers. There was more playing of games and less studying of lessons; more joyful noise and less bedtime curfews.

I spent my time with the children, playing with them, even though they did not know I was there. Josef was one of the bigger ones and was getting too

rough with the little ones. *Be careful Josef,* I said. *Be gentle with Oscar. He likes to play with you, but remember that he is much smaller.*

Rosina was a pouter. If she didn't get her own way she would just sit down and pout. I sat down beside her and said, *Rosina, Rosina, you are so pretty. You have such a pretty smile. I do not see it now. Where did it go?* She heard me. The pout was replaced by a questioning look. Then a smile appeared and soon she was up playing again.

Louisa was crying. *Why are you crying?* I asked. I sat down on the floor beside her and wanted to put my arms around her, to comfort her, but I knew I couldn't. She must have heard my question though, because she reached down and touched the scrape on her knee, trying to look at it through her tear-filled eyes. *Oh, that must hurt,* I said. *But you are so brave. Go find Rachael. She will fix it for you.* The crying stopped even though the tears kept flowing down her cheeks. She left to find Rachael.

I continued talking to the children, helping them to be good sports, to be kind, to help the smaller ones.

"This is how children should sound, happy and noisy" commented Boris, who was outwardly jolly, yet inwardly wounded, knowing what was ahead for his dear ones.

I wandered among the children to lull their senses so they would not pick up the churning feelings of their protectors. Two weeks later, a knock on the door brought the official word. It was a gruff voice: "The children will be picked up today at noon for relocation." With a heavy heart Boris told Gretta. A chill ran down her back and her knees gave way. I automatically tried to catch her, but Boris caught her and held her in his arms until she could stand again. "We must prepare the children," he said, then added, "Only you, Rachael, and I will go with the children."

Gretta had no tears left now. They were all in the chocolates, but the great empty pit inside made her ill. She straightened herself and went about the task of telling the others. Boris started releasing the other workers, giving them a chance to go hide someplace.

I found Rachael with the children and said, *Gather them all in the great hall and start singing.* I knew that singing is a good way to ease tension and lift the spirits.

While they were singing Gretta came in and whispered to Rachael, "When you finish this song I have an announcement to make. Just keep singing. We want no panic. Do you understand what I am saying?" Rachael paled. Gretta put her arm around her waist and whispered, "Keep singing . . . Keep singing." Rachael noticed the bulging bag of chocolates in Gretta's hand.

The singing continued. Rachael waved her hand in rhythm to the song, but her mind was going back, remembering the document in her personal file about the basket left on the orphanage steps—her basket. She was only two months old. Of course she could not remember that, but the story was there in her file. She knew no other life. This place had always been her home. For 26 years she had grown to love the walls, the doors, the rows of beds, and the giggles when the lights went out. Now she was leaving it. One of her greatest joys was the music in her life, and now she was going to lead the singing children from their home—her home—to a most unthinkable place. The empty space in her stomach was nearly more than she could bear.

I stood as close to her as I could to calm her and give her the strength she needed to finish the singing. *Smile at them*, I coached. *Let them see and feel the depth of your love for them. You do it so well.*

When the song was finished, she heard herself saying, "Children, Aunt Gretta has a very important announcement to make."

Gretta stepped up beside Rachel. I stood between them. Oh how I wanted to put my arms around them.

"I have a wonderful surprise for you!" Gretta said, "We are all going on a picnic to the country!" The children clapped and squealed. Gretta continued, "We are going to have a most wonderful day. We will take a train ride and have a chocolate treat." Now the squealing was joined by jumping and dancing. "Now lets sing as we march all the way to the train." As they filed out through the door I noticed that the guard had turned his head away. He was not looking at them, but he saw the bag in Gretta's hand and pointed at it. Gretta stopped. "It is just a treat for the children on the train," she explained. The guard nodded to let her pass. Suddenly she stopped and looked at the guard, "Would you like a treat too?"

No, Gretta! I shouted. She quickly turned and continued with the children.

I looked at this young guard, a soldier doing his duty, acting on orders from his commander. He was of an average build, a regular looking fellow. *Your name is Frederick,* I said to his mind. There was no response so I addressed him as his mother would have done, *Freddy, Freddy Hentschel!* His head tipped to one side so I knew that he heard me. *What is going on here?* I asked.

He bowed his head. "This is my job."

You know where these children are going?

"Yes, I know, but there is nothing I can do to stop it. I'm just a plain soldier carrying out orders." He paused and then his thoughts flowed again. "I cannot look into the eyes of the children."

My heart went out to this young man. I reached forward and gently touched his arm, sending a warm glow through him. I saw a tear escape and roll down his cheek. He slowly turned his back to the string of children.

How can I stop this massacre? I do not know. This is far beyond my experience and capabilities. My counselor had told me that there may be problems I could not solve. This is one of them.

Boris led the way, like the Pied Piper, marching and singing as all the children danced and jumped, sang and laughed along behind him.

At the train another guard grabbed Boris by the arm. "Adults are not requested to go, just the children."

Boris looked him straight in the eyes. "We have chosen to be resettled with the children."

The guard shrugged and stepped back. *Ha!* he thought, *they think they are being relocated to a new orphanage.*

Speaking to him I said, *Your name is Gottlieb.* There was no response. I stood closer to him and called his name again, *Gottlieb Schubert.* There was still no response. I wondered what had happened in his life to deaden his conscience. Looking closer into his eyes, I could see no shine, no life, only unconcern. It reminded me of a picture I once saw of a tiger—the eyes told the same cold story. I was saddened and told myself that I must remember to come back to him. I pray that my angel experiences will teach me how to separate the deed from the doer.

When I arrived at the train, Boris was still helping the children step across the foot-wide gap between the platform and the train. All one hundred of them, then Aunt Rachael and Aunt Gretta, and finally Uncle Boris stepped into the car. The children rushed to the slatted sides of the boxcar to look out, each vying for a place to see.

As the train swayed down the track little Louisa asked, "Aunt Rachael, when will we get there?"

Rachael smiled. "In a couple of hours I suppose." Louisa was satisfied with the answer and pushed her way back to join in the children's delightful squeals as they peered out through the spaces to see the beautiful country side pass by. The children were laughing, singing, and looking forward to a picnic. Most had never been in the country; never had they had a train ride before.

After miles and miles of country had passed by, Gretta spoke up in a cheerful voice, even though her heart was heavy. "Children, I have a wonderful surprise. I have a special treat for each of you. A nice piece of chocolate candy." She began passing them out, one to each child. *Oh, what am I doing?* she thought. *I hope this is right.*

"May I have another piece?" asked Josef.

"Not yet," answered Aunt Gretta. "First I must

make sure that everyone has a piece. We don't want to leave anyone out, do we?" Josef was satisfied and took another nibble from his chocolate. Some of the children gobbled the piece of candy down in one bite, but many of them just nibbled away to make it last a long time.

When all the candy had been delivered, Gretta watched to make sure everyone had a chocolate. When she was satisfied she sat on the floor with one more piece in her hand, for herself. Closing her eyes she prayed softly, "Please forgive me God for what I have done." Tears continued to flow down her cheeks; she did not bother to wipe them away.

She watched Rachael gather many children in her arms. Little Louisa spoke up, "Aunt Rachael, I am getting sleepy."

"Lean back and rest," she answered, then noticed that several of the children were already asleep. "In fact, I feel rather sleepy myself," she told Gretta. "It must be the rocking motion of this old train."

Gretta knew why her special friend Rachel was getting sleepy, and it pierced her heart.

I assured Gretta that she had done the right thing.

After another hour or so, Gretta got up and wandered through the crowded children as best she could. She saw them, each one peacefully sleeping. Some lying on the floor and some sitting, some leaning against each other and some in each other's arms. Their grey orphanage dresses and trousers shouted a somber message of their past lives, but Gretta knew that the sweet tender bodies beneath that grey were angels.

16

Even Boris was asleep. She smiled at the way he sat sprawled with children all over and around him, his big arms encircling as many as he could. He looked like the story tellers of old with children perched all over, listening to his story. He had such a way with children; he drew them like a magnet. So often they had flocked to him for stories, and sat wide eyed listening to the adventures they could only dream about.

I wondered what story he was telling them before he fell asleep. If he dozed off first, they must have giggled.

Gretta found Rachael awake but nodding. She moved little Louisa over and sat beside her friend. "Rest your head on my shoulder, Rachael," she whispered as she gently touched her cheek and pulled her closer.

"Thanks Gretta," she murmured. "I don't know why I am so slee . . . py."

"Just rest awhile. We have had a very busy day." Gretta's mind wandered back to the years of their friendship. Rachael was always so musical. There was always fun and singing when she was around. She was one of the orphans, and had always lived in this orphanage. That is why she identified with the children so well. They loved her so. *I love her too,* Gretta thought.

Gretta's face was dry now—she had no more tears to shed. The train jiggled and swayed along the tracks as the beautiful countryside swept by. Inside the car there was silence.

Gretta's thoughts went back over her own life. Her childhood was especially happy. She could still feel the thrill of running through the trees in the Black Forest. Those were carefree days. Once she had found a little bird with a twisted leg and had taken it home with her. Caring for that bird gave her the desire to become a nurse. "These children never ran through a Black Forest. All they ever ran through was the orphanage. It has been their home. Oh, how I have loved them."

Gretta looked around the silent car one more time. When she was satisfied that all were very fast asleep, she put the last piece of chocolate to her lips.

Angels can weep, and I wept, leaving a teardrop on the cheek of time.

I left my R^2 at the top of the furnace stack that had been cheated out of a train load of angels.

3

Life is like a mirror:
If you frown at it, it frowns back.
If you smile, it returns the greeting.
—THACKERAY

GOLDEN DAFFODIL MAGIC

Jim Justin purchased daffodils from the little corner market on May and Moss streets. Many water buckets of flowers were lined up along the window outside the shop. Jim stopped there every Friday after work to purchase flowers for his wife. The daffodils were in full bloom and their yellow heads looked warm and cheerful. He smiled at the clerk who wrapped their stems just as she wrapped them every Friday evening. She liked his distinguished look, especially those grey curls peeking out under the brim of his hat. *He has never missed a week for the past three months,* she thought to herself.

Jim thanked her with his usual nod and smile and left the store. She noticed as he moved toward the bus that his shoulders stooped and his step was a little slower now than it had been a few months ago, which made her believe that there was some sort of problem.

"He is so thoughtful of his wife," she told the cashier, "I wonder if she is ill . . . or maybe," she added, raising her eyebrows, "he is in big trouble with his wife. From my experience in selling flowers," she grinned, "I have found that it takes a lot of flowers to soften a heart and gain forgiveness."

"Seriously though," interrupted the cashier, "maybe his wife died."

The grin disappeared.

I followed Jim to see if there was something I could do to help him. *Jim*, I called, but he did not respond. *Jim Justin,* I called again. This time he only paused and I saw a frown appear. *He is not very receptive,* I thought. Jim climbed up the two steps into the bus and sat in the closest vacant seat. After he had settled himself down and arranged the daffodils in an upright position between his knees, he closed his eyes and relaxed to the swaying motion of the bus. His reverie was interrupted by a little sob, at least he thought it was a sob. Then he heard it again. His left eye peeked out to the side, and he saw her, a teenager, trying valiantly to keep from crying. *I wonder what she is so sad about?* he thought. He closed his eyes again, wondering if he should say something to her. Automatically, I reached over to nudge him on the elbow. He jumped. He jumped as if he was shocked. I was surprised. I couldn't believe it. He actually felt me touch him. *I can do that? I can give a little shock with my touch?* I tried it again, and again he responded. He opened his eyes and looked over at her. She had short cropped blonde hair that circled around a dainty pear-shaped face with a quite prominent nose, and red eyes all swollen with tears. She noticed his glance

20

and turned her head away toward the window.

"I do not wish to pry," Jim said, "but I am sorry that you are so sad." He heard another sob as her shoulders began to shake. "Maybe if you could talk about it . . ." Her shoulders stopped still and she wiped her eyes with her fists.

"Here is a clean handkerchief," he offered.

As she took it she saw that it was a very nice handkerchief with *JJ* initialed in the corner.

When her eyes and tear-stained cheeks were dried, a faint smile crossed her lips. She whispered a timid "Thank you." She blew her nose into that soft white linen and Jim winced.

"Now what is wrong, little one?"

She hesitated, wondering if she should tell him. Finally she took a deep breath and said, "My father died." And the sobs began again.

"I'm sorry," he spoke so softly and thought, *What does one say? What can I say to ease her grief?* She regained control of her weeping again and gave another blow into that proudly owned monogrammed handkerchief. *It's getting some good use,* he thought. I nudged him again and suggested that the handkerchief would be a good way to open the conversation, and then get her talking about her grief.

"That hankie sure came in handy today." Jim grinned and she chuckled a bit as she noticed it all wrinkled up in her hand. "Notice the JJ in the corner? Those are my initials, I guess you knew. I am Jim Justin."

"My name is Sara," she answered, "and thank you for the use of it. Fists don't wipe so good."

"I am very sorry about your father. How did it hap-

21

pen? Of course you don't have to tell me if you don't want to."

"Oh, I don't mind. It was just a freak accident. He was doing something with piping and it all blew up in his face. That is all I know." She paused as she caught her breath, then continued. "My mother is so strong and comforts my brothers and sisters. But I know that she must be hurting so much inside." As the conversation continued Sara became more calm as she spoke of her family. Then she noticed the daffodils.

"Your flowers are very pretty," she commented. "Who are they for?"

"They are for my wife."

"What a lucky woman," she said. "Do you buy her flowers very often?"

"Yes, every Friday on my way home from work I pick up some flowers for her."

"You must really love her."

"That I do." Then he added softly, "And I always will."

"My father used to bring flowers to my mother, but not every Friday like you do," she chided. That thought touched Jim to the core, and made him wonder, *Who will bring her flowers now?* Sara thought of it at the same time and turned her head away.

I gave him a big nudge and suggested the flowers and he caught on right away. He was becoming very responsive to my whisperings now.

"Would you take my flowers to your mother?" he asked.

"Oh, I can't do that."

"Sure you can. I would like you to."

"But they are for your wife, and she will be expecting them."

"Please take them," Jim said as he handed them to
Sara. She shyly accepted the flowers and caressed the
bright yellow petals.

"They are so beautiful," she said as she gently
hugged them to her chest. Jim smiled at her act of
tenderness. "My mother will love them," she added.

Their conversation continued light and friendly
until her bus stop. Sara smiled at him and was gone,
along with the daffodils and his handkerchief with the
JJ on it.

As the bus continued on its route, I could see that
Jim felt pleased that he had eased Sara's heartache for
a short time, and perhaps her mother's too. I wanted
to reward him, but not shock him with my touch. *How
do I do that?* I thought. Gently, I lay my hand on his
shoulder, and it worked. A warm glow developed in
his chest and I saw a faint smile on his face.

Jim left the bus at the next stop and slowly made
his way up the hill to the cemetery where his beloved
wife lay.

Angels can smile, and I smiled, not only pleased
for Jim's response, but also because I had discovered
two new skills; the ability to create a shock by quick
touch and a warm glow by a gentle touch.

I planted my R^2 on her headstone in place of the
flowers.

4

Time is too slow for those who wait,
Too swift for those who fear,
Too long for those who grieve,
Too short for those who rejoice;
But for those who love, time is eternity.
—HENRY VAN DYKE

WHO ARE YOU?

I was drawn to a modest little home sitting pictur-
esquely in a horseshoe-shaped valley which echoed
the curve of the St. Mary River. A mother and her two
children were part way through a busy day. I do not
know why I was drawn to this scene, but I stopped to
observe.

"Patsy, get me a diaper."

"Patsy, pick up that doll before the puppy chews
it."

"Patsy, just wait a minute and I will help you."

"Patsy, come pick up that pin for me."

Patsy this and Patsy that . . .

These requests continued, and little Patsy willingly
obeyed. She was a sweet bubbly girl, barely two years
old. The route to the clean diaper pile was quite famil-

25

iar to her. The new baby was someone she marveled at. She loved to kiss his soft fingers and his fat cheeks.

Yet Patsy was still a baby herself, but I could see that this new baby took most of Mother's attention now. The loving bigger sister didn't mind because she loved her new brother too. Mother called her a 'big helper,' whatever that meant. The tone of voice was happy so she guessed it was all right.

Ranch life was a busy one where the jobs out-numbered the hours in the day, so it was usually the 'squeaky wheel' which received the immediate attention. Patsy was not one of them. She was such a good-natured little thing that she hardly needed any attention at all. She was always around where her mother could see her and was a good little helper to run errands.

Good-natured children are often neglected, I decided. *This precious daughter requires more atten-tion than she is getting. Perhaps I can help.*

It was on one of these regular days when Patsy's mother was leaning over the crib tending the baby, when she happened to notice her two-year-old coming with a new fresh diaper in her hand.

See your daughter, I whispered.

Mother turned immediately, and wondered what caught her attention. She looked straight at Patsy. For the first time in days she actually stared at her daugh-ter. *Golly, she's cute,* Mother thought. *How fast she is growing.*

The new hard-bottomed shoes caught her eye and then the lacy stocking tops that curled down over the laces. The chubby legs and the dimples in her knees next met the gaze.

26

I impressed the mother with the thought of her child's sweetness, then touched her conscience with, *What nice things have you said to your sweet little daughter today?*

The mother looked stunned as the recording of her words played back to her: "Patsy get a diaper, pick up that doll, just wait a minute, pick up that pin." *I haven't said one nice thing to her this whole morning,* she realized. "Come to Mother, Patsy," she said.

As Patsy approached, the mother kneeled down on the floor and looked closely at her. "You are so beautiful," she said softly. With that sweet face cupped in her hands she noticed, again, the zillions of tiny hairs in the soft skin, the shape of the rounded chin, that sassy soft brown freckle in the gentle nook of the nose where she loved to kiss, and then the eyes . . . "How blue they are," she marveled. Their depth eluded her. She looked deep, and then deeper, but could not reach the bottom. A strange feeling came over her as I attempted to give her an insight into a previous life.

"Who are you?" Mother whispered. Time seemed to stand still. It was like looking deep into the heavens on a clear starry night; there was no end. "What is hidden there that I cannot see . . . but I can feel . . . Timelessness? Greatness?"

Then a realization of guilt overcame her. "What a precious child you are." She picked her daughter up, folded her in her arms, and held her tight. "Forgive me," she whispered, "you are a treasure and I promise to be more thoughtful from now on." Tears filled her eyes as she continued to hold her daughter tightly until wiggles won a release.

Patsy ran to play with the puppy and the mother

watched. *What is hidden from my sight?* she thought. I continued to give her an insight of pre-mortal life.

"Have you existed before?" she questioned Patsy. "Could it be that we coexisted together? Perhaps I agreed to be the mother and you the child. Perhaps I agreed to come forth first to prepare a way for you. Maybe your spirit is older than mine, and wiser. Whatever is there is veiled now, but I cannot help but wonder. I nearly feel guilty for prying."

I reminded her of an expression she had heard: *God doesn't manage his world with armies, but with beautiful babies. When something needs to be discovered, truths revealed, or wrongs righted, He sends a baby into the world.*

Then I suggested Mary to her. *Yes, there was Mary, the mother of baby Jesus,* she thought. *Oh, how she must have looked deep into His eyes, this time knowingly, yet wondering what great promises and sacrifices lay within. He had come at a time as that.*

The mother turned again to her daughter. "Oh, my little Patsy, have you come for such a time as this? I wonder what your future will hold?"

Angels can agree, and I agreed. Babies do come for such a time in history as needed.[10]

I put an R^2 on Patsy's soft brown freckle to remind her mother to say nice things to her children every day.

28

5

*Friends are angels who lift us to our feet
when our wings have trouble
remembering how to fly.*
—UNKNOWN

FOR THE GOOD OF THE CHILDREN

Divorce is ugly, and Connie felt ugly. I could see that she felt her life was shattered, that her life was empty and vulnerable. She was afraid and close to giving up, but I would not let her; she had two children to care for. I could read the turmoil going around her head and her heart. Her tall and slender figure had buckled down in sorrow. Her usual bright blue eyes were red and puffy, and her long wavy hair was pulled up in some sort of modern twist.

"How could he leave us?" she cried. "What is there about me that drove him away? What was there that I should have done, or what was there that I shouldn't have done? He is a beast." Then she yelled out from the very depth of her frustration, "I hate him, I hate him. I will never speak to him again." Her shoulders shook with desperate, uncontrollable sobs.

"Mom, I heard you. Do you hate Dad?"

"Yes, and I never want to see him again! How could he do that to us? We must all hate him for leaving."

I touched her knee and gave her a little shock to get her attention. *There must be no hate,* I told her. I could see she got the message, because she sobered up immediately and gathered young Bobby in her arms. "I am sorry I said 'hate.' That is a word that should not be said, and a feeling that should not be felt." She wiped her tears on the tail of his T-shirt and smiled at him. "Please forgive me."

He put his eight-year-old arms around her neck and kissed her wet cheek. "I love you, Mom," he said gently. Then he added, "but I love Daddy too. I don't want to hate him." The eight-year-old was confused, yet he tried to console his mother. "It is my fault he left; he had to yell at me all the time. I couldn't do anything right."

"NO, no it wasn't your fault Dad left," Connie insisted. "He was just angry at everything."

Just then Connie's teenager, Lori, walked through the doorway. "I just saw Dad leaving with his suitcases—where is he going? He just gave me a little wave and jumped into his car and screeched down the street."

"He moved out," was all her mother could say.

The girl looked shocked. "Forever? Mom? Forever? What are we going to do? Where will we get money? I HATE him for this!"

Bobby spoke up, "Not s'pose to hate. Mom said so."

"But see what he has done to us? Left us! It's my fault. I know it," Lori said as she threw her math book on the couch. "He didn't like the way I dressed.

He hated my sloppy clothes, but I didn't care. And yesterday he even yelled at me because I was late getting home from the mall. I just paid no attention, and walked out of the room while he was still talking to me. It is because of ME that he left."

"No, no it wasn't your fault either. Maybe it wasn't anyone's fault. He just seemed to be finished with being a husband and a father and wanted to get away." Then her voice wavered. "I don't know why. It just happened."

Several weeks went by and their attitudes worsened. Lots of complaining and accusing filled the home; the mother as bad as the children. "If Dad was here, it would be different. . . . If Dad this, and if Dad that." Hate for Dad and blame for each other seemed to be building up. Lori complained because she couldn't get the new pair of jeans she wanted. Bobby complained because he couldn't fix his bike by himself. "Where is Dad when I need him?"

I tried to reach the mother but I could not; she was becoming too bitter. *There must be a way,* I thought. Then I remembered Dr. Dirk, a family counselor, who could talk to her. *His conscience will be easy to reach because he is sensitive to inspiration.*

Better go see what is happening at the Murphy home, I told him. *That mother is struggling. There is a lot of complaining going on there. She should not allow her children to complain against their father. Not for the good of the father, but for the good of the children.*

Dr. Dirk caught on in a hurry and arranged for the mother to come into his office. He was gentle looking, as most counselors are. His eyes gave the message of trust. Connie felt that right away.

"You have been alone with your children for several weeks now," he said. "How is it going?"

"Oh, we are doing fine." That wasn't the truth but she was embarrassed to let the doctor know just how terrible it really was.

"I saw your daughter last evening at the mall. She didn't look very happy," the doctor said.

"Lori is having trouble at school. She doesn't seem to get her homework done lately. Her dad isn't there to help with her math. She complains all the time about his being gone." Tears formed in Connie's eyes, and she knew she was losing it.

"It is not good for her to complain about her father," he commented.

"I know, but we all complain. It is so hard. How could he do this to us? He was always such a great husband and father, and now he doesn't want us anymore." She hid her face in her hands as the tears began to flow.

"He has had a battle going on within himself too. Did you know that?"

That surprised Connie. She stopped thinking about her own griefs and looked questioningly into Dr. Dirk's eyes. "What are you telling me?" she asked.

He continued. "When men reach their late forties and early fifties, they go through a change just like women do. It is not the same, of course. They begin to wonder if they have been very successful in their lives. They realize that they are not so young anymore and that time is flying by too quickly." He paused. Reading the questioning in her eyes, he continued. "Men are

sometimes concerned about three areas of their lives and usually try to change one of them. Sometimes they may change two, or even all three of them."

"What are they?" Connie asked. He really had her attention now.

"They may have a desire to change homes, change occupations, or change wives." Complete silence filled the office.

"He chose to exchange me," Connie whispered. "Why me?" She was stunned. Dr. Dirk was silent. He could see the hurt in her eyes, and he sympathized with her pain.

"What were the other two you said?" She wanted to know her competition.

"One is change of a home, and the other is a change of a job," he answered.

I helped Connie search her memory for clues.

"I remember," she said, "my husband did complain lately that he was tired of our old house and wanted a new one," she recalled. "And he often spoke of changing jobs. He felt he was getting older and wanted something less strenuous."

"You see, all three—"

Connie cut in. She hardly heard what he was saying. "I should have agreed to go look at the house that caught his eye, but I liked my old home and had everything so cozy. I told him I didn't want to change." She hurried on, "And I remember him reading the job openings in the newspaper, but I told him to stop that because it made me feel insecure."

"Talking with him about his feelings would have been better than telling him of your own."

Connie nodded and lowered her head.

"But that is a bygone now, so do not dwell upon it," the doctor cautioned.

Connie did not raise her head.

The doctor said a little prayer in his mind asking, *Please help me to say the right things to help her.*

I was there to help him. It is impossible for counselors to know all of the answers. The wise counselor depends upon inspiration to guide him in serving others. I gave him some thoughts and he continued.

"There are some things I would like to suggest to help ease the situation at your home. May I share them with you?"

"Please do. My home is so unbearable; no one is happy."

"May I recommend three things you can do to make your home a happier place for your children."

I could see that she was open and ready to receive direction.

"The first one," he continued, "is to remember to say your prayers." He paused, then added, "or if not prayers, take time to be still and ponder the situations of your life and how you can come to a peaceful solution."

"I used to do that, but lately I have wondered why. What good did it do?"

"Try it again," he encouraged. "You will find that you will receive inspiration as well as comfort if you do this regularly—daily or even several times a day, when you feel the desire." Then he added, "Encourage your children to do the same. Say family prayers together or sit in peaceful counsel so they can hear your thoughts."

Connie listened attentively.

"My second suggestion," he continued, "is to take time to read. Read good things. There are good histories, autobiographies, classics, fictions, adventures, and scriptures. Yes, don't forget the scriptures. They can give you answers to your problems and solace to your soul."

"Where can I find time for that? Raising a family alone takes ALL of my time."

"I realize that, but try it. Make time for reading. It can ease your mind for short periods of time."

Connie wondered when she could do it, but she knew that she must try.

"Now for the third and most important of the three." Dr. Dirk paused and looked into her eyes, then continued at a slower rate so every word could be heard and understood. "Do not let your children complain about their father. Not for the good of the father, but for the good of the children."

"But how could he do this to us?"

The doctor heard her old complaining voice again, so he softened his own voice. "I know it is hard to understand, but it is not good for the children to have bad feelings toward their father. Children basically love their parents, unconditionally, so this love must be encouraged, no matter what has happened. What is done is done. It is the children, now, who must be protected and lifted and encouraged."

"But, how can I? My attitude is as bad as theirs." she blurted out helplessly.

"Then you must be the example. You must not complain yourself. Remember, it is not for the good of the father, it is for the good of the children. Do not let them harbor those kinds of thoughts."

"I understand what you are saying, but it will be hard."

The counselor caught the change in her voice and realized she was truly listening. "Yes, it will be hard," he echoed, and then asked, "but is it worth it?"

"Yes, it is worth it." After a pause she added, "I will try it."

"You mean, I will DO it?"

"Yes, I will DO it."

"Good! You will find that your family will be happier and better adjusted. Do not let them forget to send their father a card on his birthday, and on Father's Day. Tell stories of the good times, the funny times, and the happy times. Do not let their complaining take over to spoil the new happy spirit that will be in your home."

Connie nodded her head in agreement. She could clearly see the inspiration of his words and knew the path which she must take now.

"Do you remember these three things?" The doctor's tender words broke through her thoughts.

Connie smiled. "First, remember my prayers," she said as the doctor nodded. "Second . . ." she paused.

"Good books," he prompted.

"Yes, good books, read good books," she echoed. "And third, do not let the children complain against their father."

Dr. Dirk, with a smile, joined her in a singsong voice, "—NOT FOR THE GOOD OF THE FATHER, BUT FOR THE GOOD OF THE CHILDREN."

Connie smiled back, and they chuckled together.

Angels can chuckle, and I chuckled with them. And

I chuckled later, by myself, pleased to realize that I can approach someone through another. Dr. Dirk's open conscience allowed me to help him to help another.

I left three golden R^2's above Connie's front door to remind her of the three important rules in making a happy home.

6

*Miracles seem to me to rest not so much
upon faces or voices or healing power suddenly
near to us from afar off, but upon our perceptions
being made finer, so that for a moment our
eyes can see and our ears can hear what is there
about us always.*
—WILLA CATHER, 1876-1947.

PLEASE STOP THE WIND

The wheels on Marci's bike spun rapidly as she pedaled the five miles to Kimball, a small neighboring farming community. "Sue, Sue, I'm coming to see you" was the rhythm of the tires on the road. She and Sue had been best friends since they were in third grade. They were still best friends, but not neighbors anymore. Last Christmas Sue's family had moved from Aetna, another small farming community. That was during the girls' junior year, and now today, they would finally get together again.

Wearing shorts and a T-shirt, with a backup windbreaker outfit in her backpack, Marci made an early start this warm spring morning. The wind felt refreshing as it whipped around her legs and through her long straight, dark brown hair. The sun felt especially warm on her back as she rode along the country lane. Snow still filled the ditches on both sides, but the road was dry in most places. With care she could miss most of the puddles.

The singing of several meadow larks surprised her. Their songs joined in with the rhythm of the tires, "Sue, Sue they're singing for you." These sentinels of spring flitted from branch to twig and to fence post, continually announcing the arrival of spring. Their flashing yellow feathers caught Marci's eye.

I do not know why I followed along after her. Everything seemed to be in order. Maybe it was because I have many great memories about riding my own bike. A gold chromally two-wheeler with balloon tires and a banana seat was the rage of my young days. Could I ever do a "wheely" on it! So here I was following along with Marci trying to feel the thrill again.

Marci reached Sue's house by ten, but by noon heavy storm clouds started forming in the north sky. It was threatening enough that she decided it would be wise to start for home. The friends said their good-byes and Marci was on her way. After about a mile, the advancing storm wind hit her head on. She stopped and pulled her wind breaker out of her pack. She was glad she had remembered to bring it. Feeling much warmer, except for the sharp cold wind on her face, she ducked her head and peddled on.

Another mile passed by. Her legs began to ache from pushing the peddles so hard. *Breathe deeper,* I told her, *so your legs will get more oxygen.* She responded immediately.

Marci noticed that the meadow larks were not singing now. *Where are they?* she wondered, *Where could they run for cover?*

I told her, *Birds cannot see the storm coming Marci, but they are very sensitive to the temperature and pressure changes. Feel assured that they are safe. Probably, they are perched under cover with their heads tucked under their wings.*

Fighting that wind for another mile was hard work for Marci. She could not seem to get enough oxygen down to her legs even though she was puffing hard. A little prayer formed on her lips as she rode along. "Please stop the wind so I can get home." The wheels continued to turn and the wind continued to blow.

"I am only half way home and my legs are killing me," she complained. A turn-out on the road appeared so she stopped for a rest. Leaning on her bike she uttered another prayer, amid gasping breaths. "Please, please stop this wind," she whispered. The wind continued to blow. As she rode on she wondered if the wind was getting stronger or if her legs were getting weaker. "At this point I can't tell!" she said disgustedly.

The storm was moving in on her fast now. "I hope I get home before it begins to rain," she wished. "It may even snow! Having snow storms in April is common in this part of Southern Alberta." Even as she spoke, the soft flakes began to fall.

"That darned wind," she moaned. "I have prayed for the wind to ease, even asked twice, and it is only getting harder, and now it is starting to snow. Maybe I have not been respectful enough in my prayers." Marci rode her bike through a bare spot in the ditch and into a little grove of bushes where no one could see her. She laid her bike down carefully and knelt in prayer. "I thank thee for the many blessings I have received, but I ask one more time, please make the wind die down so I can get home. My mother will be worried. I try to pedal hard but my legs are getting tired, and I cannot breathe any faster to support them. How can I pedal harder? PLEASE stop that wind."

She pushed her bike back out onto the road and continued her ride. The snowflakes blew into her face, hung onto her eyelashes, and caught in her hair.

I was impressed by her faith in prayer, but I wondered if she was asking for the right thing. Sometimes prayers are not answered because the question was asked in the wrong way. I called to her, *Marci, I think that you are asking the wrong question.*

"What is so wrong about asking to stop the wind, or at least ask that it die down some?" she yelled back.

I could tell by her answer that she was getting discouraged. *There is nothing wrong with asking, but your prayers have not been answered. Perhaps you could rephrase them some.*

"What is there to rephrase? The wind is just too strong and I cannot keep going much longer," she snapped back. The wind continued to blow. In fact it was becoming a blizzard.

Move over. Move over, quickly, I shouted to her. I was surprised that she obeyed so quickly in her state of mind.

Suddenly a car came blindly through the flying snow, splashing water and snow in every direction. The bike headed for the ditch and tipped over in the

snowbank. Marci was covered with cold wet slush.

I thought that she was going to cry.

"I hate that snow, I hate that wind," she yelled out. "Why doesn't it stop? I thought prayers for help were answered and I need help now. Where is my help?"

I guessed that I was her help, but I did not know what to do. I wished that I could reach down and lift her out of that snowbank, brush her off, put her back on the bike and take her home. But all I could do is stand there and call out to her. *Get up Marci. Get out of there before you get too cold.*

Marci only lay back deeper in the snow. She put her arm over her face to ward off the falling flakes, and just lay there. I walked to the windward side to shelter her from the blizzard; it was such an automatic thing to do. I felt foolish and was glad that no one could see me, for how could I shelter her from the wind? It blows right through me. I squatted down beside her and coaxed, "Get up Marci, your mother will be worried about you. Come on now, your legs are rested. You can do it."

She got up, brushed herself off, got on her bike and headed down the road again.

Her legs seemed to have new life in them now, but I could tell by her actions that she was disgusted. The more disgusted she became the harder she peddled.

"Well, I will show everybody, I can do it myself," she said as she stubbornly ducked her head and peddled on. She was angry now and the adrenaline was flowing with full force. It was with this newly-found will power that she covered the last of the distance home.

She jumped off the bike, then THREW it against the side of the house, mumbling to herself about the lack of help she had received. "That wind only got stronger instead of easier," she complained.

I did help her some, but she did not recognize it. I felt that I had saved her from the zigzagging car, and coaxed her out of the snowbank and back onto her bike. She needed more. If only I could have told her the right question to ask in her prayers. I guess that I should have prayed for help myself. As I thought that thought, the answer came to me. *Yes, I am learning too.*

As Marci stomped up the steps to the back door of her home, I touched her elbow with a slight shock to get her attention. She stopped. I said to her, *God will never stop the wind, but when you ask, He will give you the strength to withstand it.*

Marci heard and pondered it for a moment. Her face brightened. "I asked the wrong question," she moaned. "I should have asked for more strength." After a pause she added, "Or I should have asked for stronger legs, instead of asking for the wind to stop."

With that new understanding she turned around, picked up her bike, and put it safely away in the garage. She was pleased with her new understanding of prayer.

Angels can be pleased, and I was pleased.

I put my R^2 on the bottom of her foot to remind her to ask for strength to push a little harder when times get tough.

7

*Noble deeds and hot baths
are the best cures for depression.*
—DOBIE SMITH, 1896-1990.

ALL IS NOT LOST

Jennie sat high on Bill's shoulder with her right arm pointing in the air. She was practicing for a dance competition at the Sheraton Hotel in San Francisco. I was proud of her, very proud.

She had come a long way. I remember when I first saw her.

Life can go on, I had said.

She shook her head, "I don't want to go on."

There are some wonderful things out there for you.

"I don't want wonderful things."

Look at yourself, Jennie, what do you see?

She turned toward the dresser mirror and gasped.

There is a beautiful smile behind that puffy face you know. Remember your mother always saying 'Smile pretty.'

"I don't want to smile pretty."

Smile.

She gave a weak smile.

Nice try, I said. *Now the eye—where is that sparkle?*

"I don't want to sparkle. I don't want to smile." She turned and flopped on the bed again.

I left her alone to cry out her grief one more time.

But I did not give up on her.

At bedtime Jennie tossed and turned. Sleep was far from her eyes. "I am so lonely! With my sweetheart gone I just don't know if I can live on." Her wedding scene flashed through her mind and she remembered the wonderful feelings. "It was like how a little newly hatched chicken probably felt when it stuck its head out of a broken shell and saw the wonders of the world," Jennie reminisced. Then Jennie's countenance fell. "Now that my love is gone I wish I could crawl back into that egg and pull the cracked end on top of me." She pulled the bed covers over her head and found comfort in the dark. But soon it became suffocating, as hiding always does, and she had to fling back the covers for new air.

Next, Jennie picked up her book to read, but the words flashed by with no meaning at all. Still, no sleep.

How can I help her? I too, reminisced. When I was small, I did not like bedtime. My mother told me that one night I said, "Going to bed is so stupid. All you do is lay there." I laugh now when I think of it, but I agree with my younger self, because if you cannot go to sleep, it really is a waste of time. My mother taught me how to sing myself to sleep; it was a little hard at first, but I soon learned to start singing as I hit the

pillow. Voila!—I would be fast asleep. Maybe it would work for Jennie.

Sing, I suggested.

"Why should I sing?" she said. "What is there to sing about?"

Try it, I coached.

Jennie started to hum a little tune, surprising herself with a few mumbled words. *What is that song?* she wondered. Her mind had turned to the song.

That is good. Sing it again, I said.

Over and over, the song went through her mind and at times through her lips, until the melody filled the space around her. In two minutes she was asleep.

I was pleased—it worked for her, too.

Jennie slept well into the morning, but again, when night came, she was sleepless.

I was so proud of her success the night before and encouraged it again. *Sing your little song again,* I suggested. *Do you remember finishing your humming last night?*

"No, I don't remember. I must have fallen asleep while humming."

You sure did. You sang yourself to sleep.

"How can that happen?"

A mind can think of only one thing at a time. It can be very busy jumping from one thought to another, but usually a song will dominate. Thinking of only the words and music will block out everything else.

"But it doesn't work on all songs, because I tried to sing a favorite modern one and I didn't go to sleep."

That is the miracle. Only comforting lullabies or hymns seem to work.

"I am so thankful that I thought to sing myself to

sleep," she said to herself.

She is still not aware that I am feeding ideas into her thoughts. Many people receive inspiration and never know the source.

Jennie's life took on a new pattern: soaring to new heights and then crashing to the old pits. As days passed the crests widened and the pits narrowed. *Now she is ready for a new suggestion,* I thought. *Dancing!*

"Dancing?" she asked "I haven't danced since before I was married because Jeff didn't like to dance."

Jeff is gone.

"Yes, Jeff is gone."

You are ready to get out into life again.

"Really? Am I?"

There is a studio on Walnut Avenue just waiting for you to join.

Finally, with shaky courage, yet with greater determination, Jennie entered the next phase of her new independent life—socializing with new people in the attractive active setting of ballroom dancing.

The studio director asked, "Why are you joining the dance studio? Do you want to go into competition?"

"Oh no!" Jennie withdrew a little. "Definitely not. I just want to try something new." I could see that she didn't want to bore him with her sad story.

Put on that pretty smile, I reminded her.

Jennie smiled prettily.

"This is Bill, your new instructor," the director said as he led her across the dance floor. Bill stood and put out his hand to her. He wasn't the tall, dark, and

handsome type you see on the dance floor in the mov-
ies, but he was a regular guy with trusting blue eyes.
He had a little mustache, a regular build, and a little
thin spot on the top of his head.

So far, so good, Jennie thought. *This was a good
move.* Six months later as Jennie waited for her dance
lesson to begin, she watched Bill dance with another
student. *He is very good,* she thought. *I feel so fortu-
nate to have him as my instructor. He is so comfort-
able to be with. In fact, he is the one solid thing in my
life right now and I look forward each week at lesson
time to be with him.*

Suddenly he was there. "Jennie, may I have this
dance?" An outstretched arm and welcome hand
reached out to her. As she reached up, his eyes caught
her attention.

He is flirting with me, she thought, and she wondered if he flirted with all his students.

Jennie teased back, "You're a flirt." He grinned.

Old dance steps were reviewed and new ones
added. There was something free and ethereal about
swirling around on the dance floor with a professional dancer. Jennie tried her best to remember all the
techniques she had learned. *His hand on my back is
firm yet gives gentle commands. The movement of
his fingers and palm tells me which step is next. The
rise and fall of his elbow under mine also suggesting
the next move.* As she pivoted under his left hand,
she felt a metamorphosis taking place, emerging a
different person. They flitted around the dance floor
like a couple of swallowtails on a warm summer day.
On the last spin Bill caught and held her "Do you
know, Jennie, that you are ready for competition?"

Jennie looked at him in awe, no breath, no blinking. Somehow she felt he was right. *Do I dare?* she thought.

He read her like a book. "Yes, you dare. I just happen to have some routines ready that we can start on next week. There are competitions coming up in Las Vegas and San Francisco next spring. How about April in Las Vegas for a warmup, and June in San Francisco for the grand finale?" Jennie's eyes sparkled yes and he knew that they were on.

I gave a thumbs-up. Her sparkle was back and she was on her way.

The next few months were spent on routines; two and three times a week they practiced for hours on end. This was serious stuff now, and Jennie did want to be good, to make Bill proud of her. He was such an excellent dancer and she learned to follow his touch, and his mood. *Could this really be me?* she thought.

They spent four wonderful April days in Las Vegas. The ballroom on the top floor of the MGM Grand Hotel was her home except to eat and to sleep. She watched, she practiced, she competed, and she drank in the rhythms and music of dance, dance, dance. Exhausted every night, she was asleep as she hit the pillow. No humming was needed. When the last song was played and the last dance was danced they flew home with trophies in waltz, Cha-Cha, and Charleston.

Sitting by Jennie on the plane Bill said, "This is just a taste of what San Francisco will be like," he informed her. "You performed like a pro," he said as he reached over and gently took her hand in his.

"Thank you, Bill, for all you have done for me. If you only knew what a wreck I was when I first came to you."

"I knew it. I felt it. It was a joy for me to see your pretty smile cautiously appear and that sparkle in your eyes shine through again. You were like a butterfly chucking that old hard shell you had pulled in on top of yourself."

"You know me too well."

"Yes," and his eyes sobered as he added, "And I like what I know." Jennie lowered her eyes as she felt herself blush. Bill noticed, and grinned.

In the month that followed she worked very hard. She found joy in Bill's arms, swaying with the Latin rhythms and gliding with the waltz. She wondered, sometimes, if he was really supposed to hold her that tight. *I'm not going to ask,* she said to herself, *because I like it.* Once his lips softly brushed her cheek and she wondered if that was part of the routine. The rush of a deep blush swept through her again.

As she fell asleep that night she wondered about Bill. The softness of his lips still lingered on her cheek. *Was it only the tango he loved? Like the song? OR, could it be . . .* She started to hum, but this time it was the Tango. That didn't put her to sleep, only alerted her senses. *Better change that song,* she advised herself. She knew she would be disappointed if it really was the Tango he loved. *Dare I hope? How often a student falls in love with the teacher. He is probably used to it,* she thought as she hummed into her pillow.

The Sheraton Hotel in San Francisco hosted the Ballroom Dance Competition in their Grand Ballroom. Competitors were arriving from all over the country. Every available space in the hotel was being used for practices and warmups.

Jennie wore new soft yellow warmup tights with a soft yellow matching skirt, full and ankle length. Her dress size had dropped two notches this past year because of her strenuous dance routines. Her muscle tone smoothed her soft skin. She was in shape and she loved the feel of it. Bill stopped when he saw her and raised his eyebrows. Jennie smiled, knowing that she bought this yellow outfit to impress him. She was pleased with his reaction. Bill smiled and took her in his arms. The warmup began.

"Relax," he said.

Jennie smiled and tried to relax while thinking, *I don't know if I am tense because of the upcoming competition, or because I am in his arms.* She tried to hum her little song to calm herself, but her little rhythm clashed with the waltz. It only took a few swirls and she was with it again. Bill gave her a squeeze and said, "That's better. You are great." She felt Bill tense up as he added, "I could dance with you forever."

Then it is the dance he likes, she thought, feeling disappointed. Without warning, he gently touched her nose with his lips. She felt new hope return.

Go ahead Bill, tell her, I prompted.

Maybe it is the dance she likes, and not me, Bill responded. *She is the student; I am the teacher. Maybe that is all it is.*

What do YOU want? I asked him.

I want HER.

Then go for it, I almost shouted.

"Jennie, it is not just the dance, it is you!" he stuttered, feeling like a school boy.

Jennie answered with her usual blush.

I smiled.

Then Bill teased. "If we win the highest points tonight, and get to dance in the final dinner show . . . will you marry me?"

Jennie stepped back and looked in his eyes. He meant what he said, even though it was in jest. Then her eyes sparkled and she teased back, "If we do NOT win the highest points . . . will you marry me?"

Bill swung her around. She put both arms around his neck as her feet left the floor.

Jennie dressed with care. She shook the Charleston dress. The white fringes danced for her, allowing the hot pink satin chemise to peek through. She put on the short tights, the soft soled leather flat shoes, the headband, long beads and earrings; all hot pink. She viewed herself in the full length mirror. "This hardly looks like me," she said out loud to herself. "I actually look like a flapper." She laughed at the thought.

As Jennie entered the ballroom there was Bill, waiting for her, with his usual grin. "Who is this bold young woman from the 1920s?" he asked as he held her tight.

"You'll wrinkle my fringe," she said with a laugh.

Bill took her hand, "We are next," he said as he gave it a squeeze. Together they watched the last of the Quick-Step. The dancers were perfect, so graceful and yet so precise.

Jennie got restless. "I have to move around," she started to walk away. Bill sensed that she was nervous and was afraid she was tightening up. He moved along with her.

"Need any scuffing on your shoes?" he asked to give her something to do. He took her emery board out of his hot pink vest pocket. He always kept it there for a last minute roughing. She sat and began sanding the soles of her slippers to prevent any slipping. Putting them back on, she wiggled her foot to feel the hard wood dance floor under each toe. Her shoes were ready and so was she. The music started, their music, *Charleston, Charleston* . . . and they were running into place to start the routine. Three and a half minutes was happening so quickly. Their energy and laughing filled the dance floor and drew applause.

No, the Charleston did not win top points, but the dancers won each other. Fairy tales do come true. All was not lost. Beautiful results happen when we step out and grow from where we are.[11]

Angels can say RIGHT ON, and I said RIGHT ON with a thumbs-up.

I placed my R^2 on the top of their wedding cake.

8

A pound of pluck is worth a ton of luck.
—JAMES A. GARFIELD, 1831-1881

TALK ABOUT LUCK!

The tall stately telephone post just outside of a small country town was the billboard. The message it bore flapped back and forth in the brisk Idaho wind. Only two nails, top and bottom, held the bright chartreuse poster announcing:

WAR BONNET RODEO
AUGUST 4-5

I do not know why I had never gone to a rodeo in my mortal life. "What the heck, now is my chance," I said to myself, "why not drop in? Maybe I could do something to help a family." But by the end of the competition, I would come to realize the value of true friendship.

I first spotted them leaning against the top lodgepole of the corral fence, so I moseyed within ear shot.

"Talk about luck! 'Twas the luck'a the draw. That's what 'twas."

"You drew Tornado?"

"Yup, I got 'im."

Cody sucked his breath in through his teeth as he said, "Maybe luck, maybe not. He's a mean one you know."

"Yeh, but if I ride 'im I'll win that purse for sure," Tex answered.

"You will. I'll bet my life on it, because I will be right there beside you." Cody and Tex were not only the best of friends, but the best team when it came to bull riding. Tex knew Cody was a top notch rodeo clown dancing around the bull in his ten sizes too big baggy cutoff jeans, and Cody knew that Tex was a champion Brahman bull rider.

Tex had won second in the Professional Rodeo Cowboy Association Wilderness Circuit bull riding event last year. Now one year later, at the Idaho Falls War Bonnet Rodeo, he was hoping to make the top. This luck of the draw might just do it for him. But being a champion doesn't always count when it comes to riding Brahman bulls. Tex knew this and depended upon the fleet-footed skills of the rodeo clown for protection.

That protection was Cody. When the rider was on the bull Cody stayed close in the background, so the bull would not be distracted. It is when that rider was off that Cody moved right in to get the bull's attention away from the cowboy. He knew how to run in and around those deadly horns, to lead the bull away, usually cheating injury and even death with every step. The fans loved his daring clowning ways, along with the bright plaid shirt and red suspenders. They especially loved the scarf-covered baggy pants which

waved around to attract the bull's attention. Other than that, Cody's job was serious business. The lives of both the rider and the clown were at stake.

As Tex and Cody walked along the arena fence they could feel the excitement rising as the fans gathered. I could feel it too. The smell of hamburgers, popcorn, and foot-long hot dogs filled the air. A soft breeze blowing through the corrals brought animal sounds and odors. Bangs on the chutes and yells of the rodeo hands echoed across the arena, where the contestants were warming up for their upcoming events.

A dozen calf ropers, with ropes in hand and piggin' strings in mouth, practiced backing their horses into the narrow space beside the calf chute. Kicking and yelling sounds came from the eight chutes where the bucking horses were being readied for the first group of riders. Saddle horses warmed up, circling the arena in soft rolling gaits, kicking dust into the eyes of youngsters hanging on the fence. The swirling dust drifted into the hair of those sitting on the lower bleachers.

Loud speakers along the spectator stands blared the rodeo announcer's voice: "Welcome, rodeo fans, to the War Bonnet Fair and Rodeo here in Idaho Falls, Idaho. It's going to be . . ."

Loud kicking noises against the worn boards in chute #2 drowned out his voice. "Seems that old buckskin in there wants to get on with the show." The crowd yelled in agreement.

The announcer continued, "The stands are packed with rodeo fans, the rodeo clowns are ready, the cowboys are in top shape, the winning purses are bulging, the winners' silver belt buckles are shining, the rodeo stock is stomping, and the bulls are MEAN." With that the fans whistled and applauded. They were ready too, especially for the bull riding event. Bull riding was the favorite of the fans. Not that they ever wanted someone to get hurt, but there was that rough-neck dangerous undercurrent in bull riding that keeps fearless cowboys competing and breathless fans cheering.

Tex settled himself beside a group of contestants on the fence by chute #7. They watched the opening grand parade of beauty queens, cowboys, cowgirls, clowns, rodeo committee members and, of course, the Mayor. All were riding by on prancing bays, duns, appaloosas, pintos, sorrels, palominos, and combinations of all the above. Arms, hands, and hats were waving and greetings were yelled out to those they recognized in the stands. When all had made their trip around the arena, the Rodeo queens, with flags waving, rode one last circle around the arena at breakneck speed.

When the dust settled the rodeo began. Bareback bronc riding was first. The buckskin in chute #2 got his wish. He threw the cowboy on the first jump. "That cowboy took a bad hit in the chute," the announcer's voice called out over the yells of the crowd, and went on to explain: "The horse reared and smashed the cowboy against the corner post of the chute. He was partly knocked off before the judges had a chance to start judging. When that happens, the contestant usually gets a reride." Voices in the crowd were yelling "Reride! Reride!" The announcer watched the judge and when the nod came he told the crowd, "It's a reeeeeeride for sure." The spectators' approval was loud and clear as hats and arms waved.

As the bareback bronc riding continued, Tex

strolled along the chutes and out the gate toward the bull pen. The bulls were bunched together, except for Tornado, who was standing alone with his tail to the far fence. It was obvious that he was at the top of the 'pecking list.' The other bulls had dared to challenge him, but lost, so now he stood alone. Tex remembered one of the worst bull fights he ever saw. A new bull was put into the pasture with several other bulls. One by one, they challenged him, until it was decided who he could beat and who could beat him. It took several days of fighting, with blood and pieces of torn hide strewn around on the grass, until each bull found place in the 'pecking list.' Now here was Tornado, in a stance that challenged anyone who would dare come near. Tex respected that and could see that the other bulls did too.

As Tex eyed Tornado, he saw that he was big. He was solid. "You proud son-of-a-gun, I'm gonna ride you." Tornado turned his head and eyed Tex. Neither moved. The hollow in Tex's stomach grew two sizes. The bull nonchalantly swished his tail.

Tex noticed the short hair and the long drooping ears and that oversized fleshy hump where the shoulder bones meet. It was very obvious how that hump curved to the left. "That is a good place to hook my leg under," he said as he stored that bit of strategy for future use. He also noticed that the two horns were asymmetrical: one was crooked, dangerously crooked. Tex remembered hearing how that Brahman favored the threatening horn and how he hooked riders with it. Tex stored that bit of information too, knowing he had to watch that horn.

Most Brahmans he had seen were red, grey, or

nearly black, but this one was red with white spots. No telling what his background was, but one thing was for sure—he had inherited all of the mean genes.

For some minutes they stood there, cowboy and bull, rider and bucker, each sizing the other. The cowboy with a championship in mind, and the bull with a reputation to maintain. Tex was fully aware that few bull riders had stayed on that back for the full eight seconds.

The sudden roar of the crowd broke the spell, and Tex turned to leave. He tipped his hat and the Brahman swished him off with his tail, as he would a bothersome fly. Tex grinned.

The calf roping and team roping events were finished. Cody was entertaining the children with his ducks and dog. After all, he was a clown and loved to make everyone laugh, especially the children. He used his little wire haired terrier, Tyke, to help hunt the ducks. A rodeo helper placed the two feathered friends out in the middle of the arena. I was surprised that they did not fly away, nor did they run; that is, until Tyke found them. Cody opened his burlap bag on the ground and Tyke herded those little quackers into it.

With the filled bag over his shoulder, Cody walked to the fence where some children had gathered. "Who would like to count my ducks?" Many hands shot into the air. A boy about ten years old didn't wait to hold up his hand; he just hopped over the fence. When he opened the sack, the ducks were gone. The sack was turned inside out—no ducks. The children stared in wonder. Cody shrugged his shoulders and turned to leave. The children were laughing, as well as the audience, for there were the ducks, poking their heads out

of the back of Cody's baggy pants. He turned to see what the children were laughing at and gave them puzzled looks. The children yelled and pointed at the back of his pants. When he turned around the ducks were behind him. They laughed and pointed all the more. I laughed too.

When he finally saw the ducks, he did a fancy dance of jumps and gyrations until the ducks flew out of his baggy pants. One got caught in the scarves and ribbons and somersaulted to the ground. Little Tyke herded them into the bag again. Cody and Tyke gave demonstrative bows: Cody's head to his knees and Tykes nose to the ground. Cody gently put the sack over his shoulder and walked to the chutes with Tyke strutting at his heels. Loud applauding, whistling, and yelling followed them.

The saddle bronc riding was winding up when Tex got back to the arena. He hardly noticed because he had his mind on that darned bull. He couldn't get that proud, nonchalant spotted giant out of his head. The bull riding was the last event of the day and he was the last of seven contestants. The bulls were driven into the chutes. Tornado was in chute #7. Would seven be a lucky number for him too? Gamblers seem to think so, and Tex felt like a gambler right now. His game was with Tornado, win or lose.

The bulls seemed anxious to get into the chutes, Tornado more than the rest. His drooling mouth was foaming and his flaring nostrils were snorting and spraying the rodeo hands. "Where's that idiot who dares to ride me?" he seemed to be asking. "Let me at him." He banged his crooked horn against the side of the chute, making sure that it was still strong and sharp. Every cowboy along the chutes heard that bang and knew that Tornado was the biggest, meanest, crookedest-horned, spinning, bucking Brahman bull on the whole Wilderness Circuit. They also knew that few men rode him for the full eight seconds, and once they were off, they knew that it was time to scramble for the fence, because that bull would make hash out of them if he had a chance.

The crowd showed their excitement for the last and most daring event of the day—bull riding. Tex moseyed over to chute #7. The bell clanked as the bull rope was wrapped around Tornado's body, just behind his front legs. That bell on the bull is like the rattle of a snake; it warns of immediate danger. When the Brahman was loose in the arena, all of the cowboys knew that clank and headed for higher ground when it rang. Now it clanked with Tornado's restless movements. The bull caught a glance of Tex to his left and aimed his ugly horn at him. The cowboy dodged and that crooked horn banged the chute gate and split the cross piece in two. The rodeo hands jumped back. "He's a mean one."

Tex climbed up the gate and looked down on Tornado. "So we meet again." The bull's tail switched, but Tex's hollow stomach was now filled with determination and had turned to steel. He was ready. He paused a little and thought of the fat purse that was waiting. As he put his leg out over the bull, Tornado reared up to meet it. Tex jumped back and said, "Hold on there, settle down now." He pulled his hat down tight on his head and put his leg out again. This time he lowered himself down behind Tornado's wicked hump. The bull's muscled back felt solid as a rock, yet

it quivered with anticipation. "That's okay old boy, I feel the excitement too." Tex wrapped his gloved hand in that bull rope, and pounded it tight with the other hand. If the rope was too loose, his hand might slip out too soon. If it was too tight, it could hang up. That is every bull rider's worst fear—getting hung up. Tex leaned back a little to test the grip. "This is going to be some journey, big guy."

Tex caught a glimpse of Cody through the chute gate and was reminded of Cody's last words of warning: "You gotta watch Tornado's left spin. I've seen him draw the rider down into that well, and pin 'em with his crooked left horn."

The fans were on the edge of their seats waiting for the last ride of the day. They were there to see the exploding action of the cowboy who dared, the clown who danced, and the bull who flouted that crooked horn.

"You ready, cowboy?" The words came from somewhere out of the air.

"Turn 'im loose!" Tex answered. The gate swung wide, cowboys scattered, and Tornado was in the air before he got out of the chute. Tex knew before that bull even hit the ground that this was going to be the ride of his life.

Tex enjoyed the motion of Tornado under him. It was a thing of beauty, like a melody. The bull's front feet off the ground and then the back ones; the cowboy's arm up for balance and then down; the switching tail back and forth, and all in rhythm with the clanking ring of the bell. Tex loved the feeling and could hear it all. Yet the undercurrent of sharp twists alerted him that this was not a Strauss waltz.

For the first few seconds of the ride Tex moved with old Tornado, never missing a beat, but the dance ended when someone yelled, "Watch out!" Tornado went into that dangerous left-hand spin. Immediately, Tex could feel the pull, tugging him to the left and down. Strain as he might, he couldn't keep the rhythm. He dug his right leg even deeper into that tough old hide and braced his thigh against that fleshy hump. But that flabby hump leaned the wrong way. Slowly he felt himself sliding down.

Where is that eight-second buzzer? He cannot hold on much longer, I thought with each jump of that bull. One leg was under the bull's belly, and the other was over his back. Tex hooked the toe of his boot behind the hump, and somehow he hung on. He was slowly slipping into the well, when he heard the buzzer sound.

"He made it. He rode you, you old rascal!" I yelled. "Is this me jumping up and down? I can hardly believe it."

The fans were cheering. "Now if I can just pull my hand free and jump to the ground in a run," Tex was thinking. For the next few seconds of the ride, Tex hung onto the side of Tornado. But his hand was caught! He was slowly slipping down and couldn't help it. He couldn't pull his hand free. The bull jerked his body back and forth. Now the fans were on their feet. Tex's boot hit the ground and his toe drug a furrow in the dirt. Someone screamed, but he hardly heard it as Tornado flipped him up into the air and down again. This time it was Cody's knee that dug a furrow in the dirt. More screams found his ears as the bull's crooked horn tore his purple shirt and raked him in the ribs.

You were right about that bull Cody, he's a mean one, I thought. In my excitement I ran out to help him get loose but realized that I could not grab him. I tried to shock the bull with all of the power I had, but my touch was not enough to faze him.

Tex could see dancing scarves and ribbons all around him and felt assured that Cody was close. *Hurry, Cody,* he thought, *this big brute is trampling my chaps. They are suppose to protect me, but Tornado's sharp hooves are shredding them.* For a couple of seconds Tex was stretched to the max, when the chaps were pinned to the ground by that big footed ox. The buckle held fast.

He felt a sharp hoof rake down his shin and realized his chaps could no longer protect him. His arm had become numb and was sure to slip right out of the socket. In fact his whole body felt numb and his foggy brain wondered if it was really him being flipped around like a rag doll. Then he thought he felt a tugging at his hung-up hand and became aware of Cody's yell.

Suddenly Tornado caught sight of Cody and spun in the opposite direction to get that crooked horn in him. The move threw Tex up and out. He was loose. But where was he? He couldn't move. It was difficult to tell which way was up or down. He tried to get up, but his legs were like rubber. He heard Tornado's bell, and frantically started crawling on hands and knees. Scarves and ribbons jumped over him, turning the bull again, but not before Tornado's crooked horn took the back of his purple shirt with it. I couldn't help him up but I gave him a shock on the bull's side to make him think it was the bull, and he spun around and headed in the direction of the fence.

Tex shook his head to clear the buzzing. As it cleared, he saw someone stretched out in the middle of the arena. His head was so muddled that he thought that it was the bull rider. *But I am the bull rider and I am here on the fence,* he said to himself. Then he noticed the bright scarves and ribbons in the dirt. Tex jumped down from the fence and fell flat on his face. His concern for his friend was strong enough to get him on his feet again and he ran to Cody.

As he covered the space in a few quick steps, many thoughts whirled through Tex's mind, *That could have been me. Cody saved my life, and now he is so still in the dirt.* His thoughts hurried on. *You were right, Cody, when you said, "Maybe luck and maybe not." That darned left-hand spin twisted my hand in the rope and I couldn't get it loose. You got it loose, but now look at you.*

Just as Tex dropped down beside him, Cody gasped for breath, coughed, shook his head, and struggled to sit up. He gasped again and then took some quick breaths. Wincing in pain, he leaned forward and held his chest. "Take it easy Cody. The bull is gone. Just lay back a minute," Tex encouraged.

Cody's plaid shirt was torn open, showing a horn scrape oozing blood. The horn had not punctured his skin, only sanded it down some. His red suspenders had snapped and his baggy cutoffs were down around his knees. Still gasping for a breath he smiled and said, "That was a heck of a ride you made, Tex. I knew you could do it."

"Thanks buddy, for the help. I thought I was a goner." Then Tex asked, "Chest kinda hurt?"

"Probably just a couple of ribs out of place," Cody answered, trying not to breathe too deeply. Then his eyes lit up and a big grin covered his whole face, "Well you're the champ, my friend."

"Yes! Yes! It was the luck of the draw." Tex stood up and yelled, "TALK ABOUT LUCK," and threw his hat high into the air.

Angels can throw hats in the air too, and I would have, if I had a hat.

I put my R^2 on that huge silver belt buckle Tex won, and another one on Cody's red suspenders, as a reminder of the value of real friends, anytime, but especially when times are tough.

9

I've found that worry and irritation
vanish into thin air
the moment I open my mind
to the many blessings I posses.
—DALE CARNEGIE, 1888-1955

THE MIRACLE OF SPRING

"Train up a child in the way he should go: and when
he is old he will not depart from it."[12] Gloria slammed
the book shut. "That scripture doesn't work, and I can
prove it in black and white. I taught my children when
they were small, but now, as grown adults, they go
their own way—drinks here, drugs there. Why?"

These are lamentations I heard from a mother who
had tried to do her best in raising her children. She
was racked with grief and disappointment.

"I feel as if I am a failure," she moaned. "There must
have been something more that I could have done. If
only I was smarter, things would be different." Gloria
slumped down into her rocker and sobbed. Her son
Jerry had dropped in to see her, and within minutes
he had turned on her and yelled, "Just get out of my
life," and then he turned, leaving in a huff.

69

She asked herself, "Have I gone too far? After all, he is a grown man with a nice family and a good job. They seem to be happy," she thought. "But he doesn't know what happiness is." She threw up her hands in disgust. "Why won't he listen to me? I have told him a thousand times what he should do."

Gloria found the scripture one more time and read it again. "Still the same," she said as she shook her head in disgust.

I tried to put some thoughts into her heart and mind, but her heart was too laden with grief and her mind too set on failure. I waited until the tide of grief had ebbed, and then tried again.

Do you love your children? I asked.

As she dried her eyes she mumbled, "Of course I do. I love them very much."

Do you want to sit in heaven with your children as a family? I asked.

"Of course I do, more than anything in this whole world. But what can I do to bring this about? They won't even listen to me anymore. I am such a failure."

Now hold on, I urged. *You have not failed. You did the best you could do. That is all that is asked of you.*

"Then, why?" she shot back at me.

Children have responsibility too, you know. I proceeded cautiously to make sure that she was following my thoughts. *You cannot be responsible for the whole of their lives. There comes a time when they must make their own decisions.*

"But Jerry is so wrong. He won't even listen to me."

Very cautiously, I said, *Should he listen to you?*

"Of course he should. I am his MOTHER!" she snapped.

Yes, of course you are his mother. Then I gently added, *You will always be his mother. But there is a difference between being a 'mother and child' and being a 'mother and adult child.'*

"What do you mean by that? I am still his mother, aren't I?"

Yes, you are his mother, but when he was a child he did childish things. He depended on you for guidance. But now, when he is an adult, he puts away those childish things and learns to make his own decisions. In doing so, he cannot blame you, nor should you blame yourself. You are not responsible for his actions anymore.

"But what if he makes a mistake?" she looked concerned.

We all make mistakes! Don't we? I asked.

"Yes," she said hesitantly, "but I thought I could save him some disappointments and heartaches."

I tried to take her mind back to the time when she was a teenager. *Do you remember, some time ago, when your father yelled at your mother?*

"My father never, ever yelled at my mother," she responded quickly.

Think back to the time when your older brother wanted to buy that new car and your mother told your father that she was going to tell him not to do it, that he couldn't afford it?

"Yes, I remember."

What did your father say to her?

"He yelled at her and told her that was not her

71

concern anymore. Now that I think of it, that was the only time I ever heard my father raise his voice at my mother. He always treated her so gently, so it surprised me to hear him treat her so."

Gloria leaned back in her rocker reviewing those days gone by. Then she caught the gist of our conversation and lurched forward in her chair. "But this is different. It is not a car I am concerned with—it is life itself, and happiness, and teaching his own children what is right and wrong."

But the principle is the same. Once Jerry is no longer a child he must be allowed to make his own decisions, as well as his own mistakes.

"Can I say nothing to him about it?"

Only if he should ask for advice, or, maybe a hint once in a while.

"I cannot handle that. I need to help him, to show him where he is wrong."

That is the way to really lose him.

"Then what can I do?"

Read the scripture again—what does it say?

Gloria opened her book and read it aloud. "Train up a child in the way he should go: and when he is old he will not depart from it."

Notice it says, 'when he is old.'

"He is old," she said, clearly irritated.

Maybe he is old physically, maybe he is old mentally, maybe he is old socially, but maybe he is not old spiritually. In the spiritual sense he is still a child. Give him some time to grow. It may take a few years or it may take a lifetime. You have taught him well and now let him grow. Your part, now, is to keep close and continually let him know that you love him unconditionally.

"What does 'unconditionally' mean?"

It means that no matter what he does or how he proceeds with his life, you still love him. You may not approve of his lifestyle, but you can still give him absolute love with no reservations. Does that make sense?

"Yes, except, I don't think he is really happy."

Know that he is happy in his own way of life right now because he does not know what he is missing. As he develops spiritually, he will learn. You may chase him away if you keep nagging. You have faithfully given him the basics to build on. Now step back and let him grow at his own speed. Be patient, and be there if he should ask for advice.

Gloria made a journal entry that night with thoughts of new understanding: "The most interesting thoughts came to me today. It was like a miracle. It came at a time when I was feeling so guilty about the way I taught my children, especially my results with Jerry. Through the years I thought that I was doing so well. I felt pleased with my children's development. But as they grew to adulthood I was surprised that Jerry did not follow through with what he had been taught.

"Just this morning we argued. After he left, I was feeling especially low and asking myself, why? Why? Why? That is when the miracle happened. My mind was opened and I understood more about that scripture that says, 'If you train your child in the way he should go he will not depart from it when he is old.' I realize now that people can be slow developers in other ways than physical. Jerry is still a child in some ways.

"Great relief settled in around me. I felt so inspired

that I put my newfound feelings in this poem, (or prose, I don't know which it is).

The Miracle of Spring R²

Just as I await the long winter months for the bare trees to send forth their blossoms and green foliage, I await for my children to blossom out in their true stature of life. I have faith that the trees will perform this miracle, so I sit, patiently and unalarmed, waiting for this event to happen. I also have faith that my children will accomplish their miracle.

I have watched my precious children grow, been happy for their accomplishments, been sad in their struggles, sat many hours at their bedsides, and yes—laughed and cried with them. I have taught them a happy way of life, then watched them, one by one, leave the shelter of their home and struggle to find their niche in life.

Now I sit and wait for them to bloom into their full stature. I sit with no alarm, but with unconditional love, patience, and faith, for I know that their long bare months will be followed by Spring.

—by Gloria

Angels can be pleased, and I was pleased.

I put my R^2 after her title "The Miracle of Spring" as a stamp of approval.

10

He who made you
expects His work to succeed
and will answer a call for help.
—HUGH B. BROWN

PUSH, PUSH, MAKE TEARS

Push, push, make tears, I urged him on. He was alive, but he was not aware of it. I knew it, because I received his weak signal being sent out through thought waves. I followed that signal and found him laying on a table in a cold military morgue. There were many there—war casualties. They arrived in droves, so many of them. Patriotic young men who were willing to fight for, be wounded for, and even give their lives for freedom. The Quonset hut for the dead was divided into two units: the front one for the new arrivals, and the back one for those who had been washed and cleaned for shipment home. Row upon row, the tables lined up in regimental order. The orderlies in the morgue tried their best to clean them up in an honorable fashion.

You are alive, I told him. *Can you hear me? You are alive. YOU ARE ALIVE!* There was no movement. *Think this in your mind, 'I am alive.'* I waited. *Yes*

I can hear you think. Think harder, I encouraged. *That's it, I heard you. Now listen to me. YOU ARE ALIVE. Move your arm.*

"C a n' t," he signaled to me.

Move your finger.

"W o n' t m o v e."

Can you twitch? Can you move anything? I asked.

"N o p e. I f e e l h e a v y, c o l d."

I could hear the signal getting stronger. *What is your name?*

He had to think on that for some time and then I received a weak signal. *Frank?* I asked.

"N o," he answered, "H a n k."

Hank?

"Y e s."

Hank, you are alive. I want to help you. I tried to speak clearly and slowly.

"W h e r e a m I?" Hank asked.

You are hurt. You have been wounded. But you are going to be OK. Listen to me, now. Can you open your eyes?

"C a n' t."

Can you cry? Try to make some tears.

"H o w ?"

Think of something sad. Think of your mother who wonders how you are. Think of the time your little dog Sam got hit by a car. Remember how you held him in your arms. You were just a kid then. You cried and cried and wouldn't let anyone take him from you. Remember?

"Y e s, I r e m e m b e r."

Remember how your tears wetted his brown fur?

76

"Yes, m y t e a r s made a puddle."

His thinking was speeding up. *Remember how you felt when you cried? Those tears just pushed right out of your eyes even though your eyes were closed. Think of that and make tears now.*

The signals were getting stronger and stronger. He was reliving that tragedy. Still no tears. *Push*, I said. *Try to push tears out just like you did for Sammy. Keep trying.*

"I am trying."

Push like you are trying to pop your ears. Think tears. Push. Push, I encouraged him on.

"I feel something wet. Is it a tear?"

I do not see one. Squint your eyes tight. I saw a slight movement and a tear drop squeezed out and ran down the side of his face.

You did it. I see it. Make some more. I will go get help.

An orderly was in the outer room attending to a new soldier. I put in his mind, *Go check the ones in the back room.*

"They are already cleaned up and ready to go," he answered.

Check again.

He left what he was doing and stepped inside the cold room and looked up and down the tables. "Everything looks fine," he said. He turned to leave but I nudged him. He stopped, kind of wondering why he should feel to check again. With a shrug of his shoulders he murmured, "What the heck." Quickly glancing at each body, he began making the rounds.

Just two steps past Hank, he stopped and backed up. Wetness on a cheek caught his eye. He took out a clean cloth and wiped the cheek clean. "Looks as if I missed your cheek, fella," he apologized. Finishing his round he disappeared back to his former project.

Hank, you did great. You got his attention. Keep making those tears, buddy.

The other orderly finished cleaning up his soldier and wheeled him into the cold room. As he was leaving, I guided him past Hank. "Woops, missed a little spot." He took out his clean cloth and wiped the new tears away, and was gone.

Buddy, you are doing great, I told Hank. *You have tears coming out of both eyes now.*

"I would smile if I could. What is your name?"

My name? R².

"R²?" he questioned. "You're square?" he teased.

Hey now, my friend, you are getting too smart with your signals. I laughed, and I could tell that he was laughing too. I found myself getting very attached to this soldier boy and prayed for his recovery. He lay there so wounded and stiff, yet we were laughing together.

My mind wandered back to World War I when I, too, lay wounded with a gouge in my leg the size of two donut holes. The scar is still there. We laughed a lot in that hospital. It replaced a lot of crying and homesickness.

The first orderly brought in his next soldier. I guided him past Hank as I had done with the other orderly. He stopped when he saw the wetness on Hank's cheeks. Now tears were running down both sides of the face. "What is going on here?" he said out loud so we could both hear him. "This is the same face I just wiped clean." Then he noticed that both cheeks were wet. "Hey, Buddy, are you making tears?"

He dashed off to find the other orderly, and explained what he had found. They realized that both had wiped that same face. They rushed to Hank's side again. More tears were escaping down his cheeks. "Are you alive?" they questioned excitedly.

I heard Hank try to say, "Yes, yes, I am alive." The orderlies only saw the sudden gush of tears.

"Did you see that? He IS alive." They quickly grabbed his name tag. "Hank Hailey," one orderly read, "Hank, can you hear me?"

Again, only I heard Hank answer, "Yes I can hear you."

"Let's get him out of here. Call the doctor." By now all four of us were making tears.

Hank was moved out of the morgue and into the room of the living.

Angels can make tears too, and I did. They were tears of joy.

I put my R^2 in place of his name on the Tomb of the Unknown Soldier in Washington, D.C.

11

A torch was given to me
that I might light the lamps of others
as I seek to see the road ahead.
—HUGH B. BROWN

LEMON AND LIME

A little family of five was living temporarily in a cabin while their carpenter father built a cabin just next door. The stay was only for one month so the family had come along to this summer playground in the Rocky Mountains. Waterton Lakes National Park is located on the Canadian side of Montana's Glacier National Park. Together, the Parks are named the National Peace Park. The three lakes are surrounded by craggy snow-topped mountains which rise straight up out of the clear blue water.

This month, for the little family, was dedicated to enjoying the outdoor life. It offered many opportunities for walking, site seeing, and especially for reading stories under the trees. Walking along a tree-covered trail, the mother would point out the kinds of wild flowers, the children would feel the spongy texture of the moss which grew on the north side of the trees, and they would all freeze in place to watch a furry animal cross their path.

I observed how the mother would help her children learn about the beauties of the earth, and make them aware of the Great Creator who made this all, just for us.

"Look at all these beautiful things," she would say. "It is important to see with your eyes, to listen with your ears, so you know what is going on around you. This awareness protects you from being deceived," and she would add with a smile, "so no one can 'pull your leg.'" The children always laughed at that.

"Pull my leg," they would echo and giggle.

They had books on Mother Goose, the Classics, and of course, the scriptures.

One of the children's favorites was *Charlie,* a story read so many times that the children had memorized it. Even though they were not old enough to read all the words, they could read the pictures. Each page was turned at the right time with no words missing.

On this particular day they chose a cozy place for reading. It was just off the trail, in a mini meadow where rabbits, field mice, squirrels, and even deer paused to check for intruders before crossing to get a drink.

The story chosen for today was about Lehi, a man in ancient Jerusalem who was told in a dream to take his family and leave the city because it was going to be destroyed.

As always, at the beginning of a lesson, the mother would have a little review and ask questions to wake up little minds in preparation for reading. With all faces turned toward their mother's, they waited.

The mother asked this question, "What are the names of the four oldest sons of Lehi and Sariah?"

"Nephi and Sam," they practically shouted in unison. "They are the good boys," they added with smiles on their faces, feeling pleased that they knew the answer.

"Yes. Why do you call them good boys?"

"Because they did good things."

"What good things did they do?" the mother continued to question.

"They obeyed their mother and father and were kind," was the quick answer.

Mother smiled, then continued, "Now what are the other two sons named?"

The children were quiet and their expressions showed that they were trying very hard to remember the other two sons, Laman and Lemuel.

Ron spoke up, "They were the bad boys."

"Well, lets say they were not really bad boys, lets say that they just did bad things," Mother said.

That was something to think about. Mother continued, "We must not think that people are bad, but sometimes they make poor choices which makes them do bad things. Now what did the other two sons do that was bad?"

"They grumbled all the time and were mean to their little brothers," was the answer.

"That is right. Should we grumble?" she asked.

"NO," was the answer in unison.

"Should we be mean to others?"

"NO," they chimed again.

"Can you remember their names? Remember,

you said Nephi and Sam were the boys who did good things, now what are the names of the other two brothers?"

It was quiet, and the mother could tell that her children were deep in thought, searching their memories for names. The names of Laman and Lemuel were hard names to remember.

Finally little Patsy, age four, got a twinkle in her eye and shouted out, "I know their names . . . LEMON AND LIME."

Angels can laugh so hard they have to hold their sides, and I did.

I put an R^2 on the sacred name of Mother; for all the mothers in the world who bless us all, including my own dear mother.

12

*Sometimes bad things happen
to good people.*

OPPOSITION

I was beginning to discover what being a ministering angel was like. Happy times and sad times, yet still I felt that I had been doing some good. But it seems that just as one starts to feel pretty confident, a new learning experience arises.

It was past midnight when a blinking light flashing the words 'drink up' caught my eye. The little street was quite dark and empty, except for a couple of cars, a dented mail box, and a stray dog who was half way into a tipped over trash can. The small shops which lined both sides of the street were dark and closed for the night. The flashing lights of the only open place of business seemed to beckon me.

I stood at the door to observe the area, and to see why my instincts called me here. The air was so thick and hazy that I could hardly see across the room. There were several small round tables scattered here and there; chairs haphazardly placed where earlier customers had left them; a lighted jukebox playing some kind of so-called music. At one table sat a man and a woman deep in discussion; their beer glasses making frequent trips to their lips. The bartender, in his cleanest dirty white shirt, was leaning on the counter talking to a customer who was hanging way off his stool. The last two people in the room were down at the far end of the bar. One of them was on the end stool, and the other man was standing unusually close beside him. Their mode of conversation intrigued me. The man standing was doing the talking and the one sitting was continually shaking his head up and down and then back and forth.

I moved in closer to observe. As I approached them, the man who was standing looked up at me and started backing away. I stopped in astonishment. *How could he see me?* I wondered. *A specific instruction was given to me that no one could see me. Yet he can see me! He saw me as I approached.* When I stopped, he stopped; when I stepped closer, he stepped back. *Why?* I wondered. He had on a dark shirt and pants. His dark hair was tidy where it stuck out from under his baseball cap. In fact, he was a handsome fellow. I could feel that he didn't like me.

"Why are you here?" he asked. I was so surprised that he spoke to me, I was speechless. Then he added, "This is my area. Get out!" The man on the stool continued to shake his head as if we were not there.

Even though I still stood in astonishment, I had the feeling that he was leery of me. I took a step toward him and he quickly took several steps backwards. *Yes, he is afraid of me,* I confirmed to myself. *Anyone would feel uncomfortable if seeing an angel, but I wondered why he could see me.*

He spoke, "This man is my friend, I have been living with him for several years now."

I walked up to the man at the bar and asked, *Is this man a friend of yours?*

"What man?" he asked me. His voice was very slurred and difficult to understand.

That man, who was standing beside you—is he your friend?

"I have no friend," he muttered.

I looked up at the other man and he was gone. *That was quick,* I thought. I turned my attention back to the man on the stool. *What is your name?* I asked.

"Huh . . . Oh my name? Uh . . . my name is Henry," he answered.

I think that you should go home now, I suggested.

"Yes, just one more drink and I will go," he blurted as he put up his hand to order another drink. The bar tender saw him and started toward the spigot, but I sent a message to him and he changed his direction to talk to Henry.

"Henry, I think that it is time to go home. Can I call a cab for you?" he asked.

Henry nodded.

I followed Henry as he staggered out the door and rather crawled into the cab. As I got into the cab to go home with him, I turned and saw that mysterious man standing under the flashing light, watching me. A chill shook me, and my senses reached out for answers.

Henry's wife Mary was waiting up for him. "Thank goodness, you are home." She looked relieved. "I was about to come and get you," she added, helping him through the door. He gave a half smile to her, staggered into the bedroom and flopped down on the bed. She took his shoes and jacket off. "You are too heavy; you can sleep in your clothes." As she covered him up she muttered, "Why do you stay so late and come home so ugly?"

"I'm not ugly to you, am I Mary?" he sounded so melancholy.

"When you drink too much you are ugly."

He mumbled something about ". . . only one . . ." and was fast asleep.

Mary shrugged and left the room. She looked too despondent to go to bed herself. She just plopped down into her padded chair which seemed to wrap around and hold her as a mother would a child. My heart ached for her. Words just did not come to me and I grappled to know what to say to her. She must have been enabling him for many years. *Does she even know what enabling is?* I wondered.

Mary, I asked, *why do you do this for him?*

"I don't know," she answered, "I know no other life. He is such a sweet man when he doesn't drink." She paused and then added, "If only he would come straight home from work. He tells me he doesn't want to do it, but he just doesn't seem to be able to stop. It is as if someone was egging him on and making him drink, yet when I pick him up at the bar, he is always alone."

I looked out the window and saw that same man standing under a tree. *Mary*, I asked, *do you and Henry have a house guest?*

"No," she answered. "The two of us have been alone since our daughter married five years ago."

Glancing out the window, I saw that the mysterious stranger was gone.

The next day I was at the bar when the working men showed up, watching for Henry to appear. Sitting in an inconspicuous place to wait, I soon saw Henry's friend appear. He walked straight to the end stool and sat on Henry's stool. Luckily he didn't see me. Suddenly he turned his head toward the door. I followed his eye direction and saw two men enter. They headed straight for that same bar stool. Obviously, they knew each other and could see each other. The two new fellows weren't dressed in black like Henry's mysterious friend; one wore blue jeans with a bright red shirt. His eyes were blue as the noontime sky. The other one wore baggy shorts. I noticed his blonde pony tail was as long as his shorts. The three of them laughed and joked as they kept their eyes on the door.

They are obviously waiting for someone, I thought.

As workers started straggling in, these three men approached them and sat with them. It was obvious to me that the workers could not see the three of them.

They are like me? I wondered. I was shocked! *Are they angels too?*

Watching closer, I observed that they were trying to get the men to drink. Turning up my hearing abilities, I found that I was right—they were encouraging the men to drink. *This is not what angels are supposed to do. They seem to represent something dark and evil.* My understanding was clearing. They were part of that army of mischievous angels who tear down the family instead of building it up. *They are like me except our*

89

missions are completely opposite; I am here to save families, I thought to myself.

As I watched their influence upon these men, I noticed a strange phenomenon. As a man lifted a drink to his lips, the dark angels would get as close to his mouth as they could and try to have a drink.[15] It was pitiful. How badly they seemed to want a taste of that liquor, but in their state, they could not. Even though they were my worst enemies, I couldn't help but feel their anguish.

One thing was comforting to me though: the angel dressed in black was afraid of me.

I was so deep in thought that I did not see Henry arrive. When I did see him, the dark angel was right there with him. I was immediately there beside him too.

Henry, I said, and the dark angel jumped back and joined his other friends. Now all three of them were staring and pointing at me. I said a quick prayer to ask for help in case they attacked me. They were snarling and hissing, trying to scare me off. I stood solidly by Henry. They did not come closer. Holding my breath, I dared to take a quick step toward them; they jumped back several paces. *Yes they are afraid of me,* I thought. *I must have more power than they.*

I turned to Henry. *Better go home,* I advised.

The three yelled at Henry, "Just one drink Henry, you can go home after just one more drink."

Come on, Henry, I urged. *Mary is anxious to see you home.* Henry got up from the stool and went home. *I actually won that battle,* I thought. I felt ecstatic. I followed Henry home and Mary was just as happily surprised.

A week later I went back to see Mary and Henry. Only Mary was there. *Where is Henry?* I asked.

"He hasn't been home for two days now. He's probably at . . . you know where." Her face looked tired and weary with worry.

I immediately went to the bar, and there he was on the end stool with the three dark angels egging him on. "Just drink one more," they would say while laughing and having fun.

I was disappointed. Now the three of them had ganged up on Henry—no wonder he had not been home. *Must I stay with him all of the time?* I asked myself. As I was pondering the problem, Henry got up and moved quickly over to two young men who just came into the bar. He took each by the arm and escorted them outside. I followed, as did the three dark angels.

Henry asked the young men, "What are you doing here?"

"Just want to get a drink, Grandpa," they answered.

Hurrah for Grandpa, I thought, *talk to them.* And he did. They talked until their legs were tired and then they sat on the curb and talked some more. Grandpa continued to explain how his life had been ruined and how their grandmother was so unhappy. "Some people can drink a little and then let it alone; others cannot," he told them. "The hard part is knowing which one you are. You never know unless you take that first drink."

Tell them how the addiction may run in a family, I prompted.

"Look at me, my grandsons, I am like my own

91

father, who was an alcoholic too. Often a weakness for this sickness runs in a family. For me, do this for me, please go home. Break this terrible chain that has run rampant in our family." The two young men seemed to understand. They finally agreed and left.

Henry, I said, *that was a wonderful thing to do.* I saw tears in his eyes.

"I do not want them to start on the path I am on. It is a never-ending one. The destination is pure misery."

It doesn't have to be that way Henry, I said. *I can show you where you can get help. You have a disease that can be cured.*

"It is too late for me. I have gone too far."

It is never too late, I advised. *Come with me now and I will show you where to go.*

"No . . . no," he said as he shook his head, then he added. "I am not proud of much, however I am proud to say that I turned those two young men away from this kind of life. I feel good about that. It's one good thing I can always remember that I did."

I tried desperately to take Henry with me and get the help for him that I knew was out there. He would not go with me. He went straight back to his favorite stool. I wished that I could do more. Henry does have his free agency to choose what his life will be. I can only suggest, encourage, help him to see the error in his ways; but in the long run, he makes the choice.

As I left the place, I took one more look back at Henry sitting on the stool at the end of the bar. His shoulders were hunched, his head drooped; he was not a happy person. The three dark angels were crowded close, trying to get a sip of Henry's drink.

Angels can be sad, and I was very sad.

I put an R^2 at the top of the door to the bar. That is not a good place. I would call it a condemned place, an unfit place, an inappropriate place—a place of doom.

Epilogue

*God often visits us,
but most of the time
we are not at home.*
—FRENCH PROVERB

"Randolf Rippenhoffer, R^2, COME HOME." I heard my name being called.

"Come home?" I asked.

"Yes R^2, come home."

"Why? Is something wrong?"

"No, not wrong."

"Is it because I could not help Henry?"

"No, you did all you could for Henry. Let him be on his own for a while. Approach him again at another time. He may be ready to listen better then."

In a firmer tone, the voice added, "You are being called home because there is someone here asking for you. They are getting impatient to meet you. They refuse to continue in their eternal journey until they see you. Please hurry home."

As I entered the brightness and loving warmth of my heavenly home, I was greeted by one hundred pairs of little arms. All embracing me, around my legs, my back and front, in fact, around every part of me, depending upon the height of the child. I recognized little Louisa right away, and then I remembered who they were. I lifted my eyes from the tops of their heads and there stood Uncle Boris. Yes, even Aunts Gretta and Rachael were smiling. My heart leaped with joy. They were all there. My mind echoed the picture of Gretta standing there by the stove making that chocolate candy, her salty tears flavoring the mixture as she stirred; and of Rachael leading the children in happy song as they marched to the train. Now look at them. They are so happy. Louisa's voice brought my wandering mind back. "What is your name?" she asked.

"My name?"

"Yes, we want to know your name," echoed the children.

"My name is R^2."

They were silent. They stared in puzzlement. Josef said, "That is a funny name."

"That is a nickname, children," Gretta explained. "His real name is Randolf Rippenhoffer."

"Randolf Rippen . . . what?"

"Just call me R^2." I said. "That is easier to remember."

"R^2 . . . R^2 . . . R^2 . . . R^2," chimed the choir of little voices.

"Children, it is time to go now." The announcement drowned out their calls.

After the hundredth hug, they were on their way. "Goodbye R^2," they called as they waved.

"Thank you R^2."

"We love you R^2."

Their little voices were still echoing in my mind when a voice broke through my thoughts. "So, you gave my flowers away!"

I turned and there stood a lovely lady in a flowing white gown. Her auburn curls fell softly across her shoulders. "Your flowers?" I asked.

"Yes, my daffodils," she answered with an accusing look, yet there was a sparkle in her eyes.

"Oh! You must be Jeff Justin's wife."

She nodded with a grin, and then added, "I laugh every time I think of his white linen handkerchief. Sara gave that one a very good workout, didn't she? You know, he was always so particular about those JJ handkerchiefs. He was never without one. He told me about Sara when he came up the hill, and apologized about giving my flowers away to her mother. Of course, I told Jeff that I understood. That was such a gentle thing to do."

I agreed, "Yes, Jeff was gentle."

She continued, "He was quite touched by the feeling of cheering Sara up a little. He told me how she had gently caressed those daffodil petals. As he told me I saw a tear trickle from his eye. I smiled as he reached into his pocket for his handkerchief and it was gone. For the first time in my life I saw him pull out his shirt tail to wipe away his tear. Thank you so much for what you did."

Then she touched my arm and said "R^2, you are an angel." She smiled and was gone.

"Me? An Angel? Yes . . . I guess I am." I stood there alone with my many thoughts: JJ, Sara, the children, Rayman, Patsy, Marci, Jennie, Tex and Cody, and Hank. "What a joy it has been to help them," I thought. "During my lifetime, I passed up so many opportunities to uplift and to help those around me. Hindsight is so good. I do wish that I had done more."

"Well you CAN do more," the voice broke in. "What are you waiting for?"

"I can go back?"

"Of course," he said with a laugh.

"Right on," I shouted and laughed, because . . .

Angels Can Laugh Too

Then the first thought that came to me was, *I wonder how Henry is doing?*

1. Testimony born by Matron of the Idaho Falls Temple, given at an area conference in the Idaho Ricks College auditorium. Elder Nelson was the visiting speaker. During his talk he invited Sister Bramhall, the Matron of the Idaho Falls Temple who was sitting on the stand, to share something with us and bear her testimony. As she spoke she told us that she knew she had a guardian angel because she knew his name and she had heard him chuckle.

2. The light in the corner of the room was a personal experience of author at the time of the birth of one of her children. Her thought of who would take care of her children brought her back to the bed.

3. "Why an Angel?" *The Discourses of Wilford Woodruff*, pp. 12-13.

4. "Angels as Watchmen and Messengers," *The Gospel Kingdom, Writings and Discourses of John Taylor*. p. 31.

5. Moses 7:28-31,37;. *Enoch the Prophet* Hugh Nibley p. 5, 189.

6. "Why an Angel?" *The discourses of Wilford Woodruff*, p. 12-13.

7. "Angels as Watchmen and Messengers," *The Gospel Kingdom, Writings and Discourses of John Taylor*. p. 31.

8. Personal experience of the author and son.

9. One line Thought of train load of children on their way to the Gas Chambers, from James A. Michener's book.

10. Genesis 44:7-8; Ester 4:14; *Faith Precedes the Miracle*, Spencer W. Kimball, quoting F. M. Bareham: When the Lord wants something done, he doesn't send armies, etc., he sends a baby into the world.

11. Author personal experience—dancing lessons and competition part only.

12. Proverbs 22:6

13. Based in part upon an experience told to author by a friend.

14. Jerusalem was destroyed in the seventh year of the reign of Hezekiah, King of Jerusalem. Shalamaneser, the king of Assyria, demolished the government of the Israelites and transplanted all the people into Media and Persia. Josephus IX, XIV, 1. p211

15. A real illusion as told to the author by an alcoholic.

About the Author

Alberta Rothe Nielson was born in Southern Alberta, Canada on Black Tuesday. She grew up on a ranch where she learned to saddle horses, drive a team, feed chickens, and milk a cow.

Berta joined the LDS Church when she was 24. She has served as both a stake Relief Society and Primary president.

After raising seven children, she went to college as a 50-year-old grandmother to obtain her engineering bachelor and master degrees. After retiring, Berta served two missions: one at the International Affairs Office in Washington, D.C., and the other in the Hawaii Reserve Office in Laie, Hawaii.

Berta now lives in Salt Lake City where she is concentrating on writing family histories and searching out her kindred dead for temple blessings.